FALLING FOR HER FAKE HUSBAND

FINDING LOVE 3

TONI DENISE

Thank you to all who have read my books and for enjoying this series as it completes. And for being patient as it did!

1

David shut his front door behind him as he walked into his house for the first time in almost a month. He tossed his standard black duffle bag near the couch and headed straight for the kitchen and a much needed beer.

He'd made up his mind not to travel anymore and had spent the entirety of the last week trying to talk himself out of "one last job" like this hadn't already been his third one. He enjoyed doing security work, and it kept him busy, but he was ready for more than just a home base. He wanted an actual home.

He worked for a security firm and had ever since he'd left the military. He had enjoyed the change of scenery at the end of every assignment for a while, but not so much anymore. Instead, he was moving to a consulting role with a lot less travel. None if he didn't want there to be.

Running a team of men from his computer would be a new interesting challenge, he thought. Couldn't be any more difficult than doing it in person since some of them never listened anyway. Those men wouldn't be on any of his teams. The one thing he'd made sure to get out of this position change aside from less travel was that he got to pick his team, no matter what.

Now though, he had two weeks of peace before he even needed to think about the next job, something he was grateful for. He was happy to get back to doing his own thing for as long as time would allow.

This was his now too. He'd bought the house from Mike not long after he'd married Kristin and had gotten a lot of furniture in the process. Mike had moved in with her, and the plan had been for David to rent, but they'd agreed on the sale instead. It also meant Mike's crazy mother couldn't come wandering in anymore like she owned the place.

He rolled his eyes at her outlandish behavior. It was a real wonder Mike had any sense considering who raised him; that woman was a challenge. She also reminded him of another mother that he hated thinking of.

Pulling another swig of his beer, he sat at the table. Thinking of that mother always pulled him back to Chloe, his wife. No one knew her here.

It had been a sham of a marriage, just him stepping up for her to provide all the freedom he could for her and the baby before he shipped out. He had been home taking leave when he popped in to see his uncle and happened to run into her.

It had been nearly three years ago, he thought. For three years, he'd been secretly married, with a child. He provided for them as much as she would allow, sent funds every month like clockwork and his insurance covered them both.

Chloe had gotten herself into a spot with Larry, a real jerk from a lot of money. She'd realized too late that Larry was an abusive piece of work; she was already pregnant. He'd offered her the security of a marriage without the man being there, and then he'd left.

The problem was that Chloe's mom was more interested in the great match than her daughter's feelings or safety. He hadn't been surprised by that, just as he hadn't been surprised when she lost her mind when she found out Chloe and David were married.

After the blowout with her mother, he'd asked her to leave with him. She'd refused, viewing herself as a burden despite all David's claims to the contrary. They'd found an apartment, David had put the deposit down and several months' rent, and he'd even gotten a few pieces of furniture before he had to leave her there.

The money, she rarely touched, was in a joint account, one of the few things linking them together. He was happy she used it when she had to, but he worried anytime she did that something was wrong. She reached out via email now and then, but it had been a while since he'd heard from her. For his part, he'd sent her his new address, as he'd done every time he moved, but he never got a response.

Chloe had always been the one that got away, except he'd married her. It was a mess. At the time, he would have accepted the full marriage and baby, but she didn't seem to want that. He did—still did, if he was honest.

His two best friends had recently gotten married and were blissfully happy. It was great for them, but damn if it didn't make him yearn to have a family too. He tossed back the last of his beer and set the bottle on the table with a sigh.

Maybe it was time to find out what Chloe's plans were and exactly what she wanted from him. He didn't want to lose her either. What he wanted was her to give the marriage a try, but how did you tell someone that when you never talked to them?

He grunted and picked up the bottle, tossing it in the trash. Mike and Kristin had invited him over tomorrow for brunch along with Macy and Daniel. He wanted to go, but at the same time, he didn't. It was hard to be around everyone so happy and committed and not have that.

Grabbing his bag, he strode down the hallway for the bedroom. Tomorrow would come soon enough, and he needed to get some rest.

After showering, he emptied his bag and pulled out his computer before putting everything away. Opening it, he checked for any emergencies with work before shutting down and calling it a night.

Sure enough, the next morning came quicker than he'd wanted. He hadn't slept well, a common theme whenever his mind was stuck on Chloe.

He opted to go for a run today; the crisp fall air was sure to help clear his thoughts, as well as the music blasting through this headphones as he tried to push the thoughts back. Usually, he could clear his mind with a good workout, and today was proving to be no different.

Running through the neighborhood that he lived in, he found himself looking at everything and everyone from a security aspect. He'd done that for too long to shut that part of his brain off, but it helped him focus. His watched vibrated on his wrist letting him know it was time to make his way back to his house if he wanted to make it to Mike's on time.

Changing direction, he circled back through the neighborhood at an easier pace, cooling down. He made mental notes of the people he passed, those who spoke and those who didn't.

Some people didn't speak because he looked scary, but he was used to that. Over six feet tall and a muscular 220 pounds, he knew people found him intimidating. Others studied him openly, wondering who he was and why he was there.

No one stood out as a threat, and he hadn't expected any. It was important to always be aware of your surroundings though. After working for some high-profile clients last year, he'd learned that neighbors weren't always who you thought they were.

His morning run had gone as expected right up until he turned the corner and could see his house. In his driveway sat an older Camry, green, with paint chipping off in places on the driver's side.

Slowing to a walk, David considered passing his house but decided to confront whoever it was head on. Walking to his house, he avoided cutting through the yard, taking the longer route through the driveway and alongside the car.

Straining, he listened for any sounds that might give him a clue as to who it was. A lady, it appeared, with brown hair was in the driver's seat, looking at something on her phone.

She wasn't paying attention to anything but her phone, or she would have seen him in one of her mirrors. He wasn't hiding; he wanted to catch a glimpse of the face.

Forcing his shoulders to relax, he wondered if it was one of Mike's ex-girlfriends come to find him. That would certainly make for an interesting brunch topic. That thought made him smile as he approached the car now from the driver's side.

Looking in the windows as he did, he noticed a small child with auburn hair peaking out from under a beanie, sleeping in a car seat in the back. A thick, blue blanket was tucked around the child. The smile he'd had was threatening to slip so he made an effort to paste it back on and seem casual as he knocked on the window for the lady to look at him.

When she turned, his heart stopped beating as the world froze. Big green eyes shined up at him, tears making them shine. The dark circles under them showed through the makeup that was obviously meant to conceal. She'd been crying and looked exhausted, but it shocked him to see her at all.

"Chloe?" he asked, as though she wasn't real.

He opened the door and held out a hand to help her out of the car. She was real, but if she was here, it meant something was wrong, very wrong.

"David." She breathed as she stood. "I'm so sorry."

2

Chloe had left in the early hours of the morning to make it to David. She hadn't wanted to be discovered and doubted anyone would notice she was gone until she was well away. It had been a tremendous risk coming here, but didn't know what else to do.

"What's going on?" David asked, taking her in.

She hated the way David only really ever saw her at her lowest points. Reaching up she pulled a finger under each eye attempting to clean up the makeup she knew had run when she'd realized he wasn't home.

He travelled for work, she knew that, yet she had come unannounced anyway. There had been no chance to ask first. Instead she had run to him, hoping he was here.

"I—"" she started and then stopped, realizing she didn't know where to begin.

"Let's go inside first; you look frozen," he urged when no words came from her.

"I have to get Sadie first." Pointing at the backseat, she felt her shoulders fall. It had been such a long day already.

"What can I get out of the car for you?"

"Just the diaper bag; it's in the front seat."

Getting Sadie out of her car seat hadn't been hard. She was so tired she didn't even stir much other than to resituate herself in Chloe's arms. David opened the front seat and grabbed the diaper bag before leading them into his house.

It was clean and simple, she thought to herself as she followed him in. Very much like she had expected it to be—modern but homey at the same time. The colors were dark, but the walls were white, giving contrast and opening the living room up to seem bigger.

Interior design had been something she always wanted to do. She had even started going to school online for it before last month. Last month had ruined everything. Her mother had ruined everything.

"Do you want to put her on the bed?" he asked, pulling her from her thoughts.

"Yes, please."

Following him up the stairs and down a hallway, she held Chloe tight as she prayed David would be willing to help them. He gestured to a room and let Chloe walk in first.

This room was so much David she almost cried. It was sharp lines, dark wood, with a poster bed in the center of the far wall. The covers were a deep, rich blue, with two throw pillows breaking up the darkness with a patterned pale blue.

"Under the covers?" he asked, ready to pull them back.

"I'm sure she will be fine on top," Chloe assured him.

He looked at her questioningly, arching one eyebrow, but he didn't argue. Chloe laid Sadie down on the bed, pulling her hat off her head as she rolled over, immediately getting comfortable.

"I'll be downstairs when you're ready," David told her and left the room.

She'd never be ready. She needed to be, but it was more of a rip-off-the-Band-Aid type deal than actually being ready.

What she wanted to do right now was curl up in the bed with Sadie and sleep the sleep of people who were safe and didn't have any cares. But that wouldn't happen, so with a deep breath and a kiss on Sadie's cheek, she turned and went in search of David.

"Coffee?" David asked as she found him in the kitchen.

"Yes, please," she said, taking the offered cup.

"I don't have any good creamer. I just got in last night, but I do have some sugar if you want that?"

"I'll be fine. Thank you though."

A small table with four chairs sat near a window in the kitchen, and Chloe walked to it, sitting in one of the chairs and waiting for David. He joined her. She'd expected he would stand and hover, waiting for an answer, but she had to remind herself it was David. He wouldn't push; he'd listen, he'd wait, but he wouldn't force.

"Why didn't you call, or email, or anything?" he asked when she couldn't find the words to start the conversation. His tone was worried yet soft and comforting as he watched her sip the coffee.

"I couldn't," she admitted. Pushing the cup away from her, she sighed again, and started to explain. "Early last month, I ran into my mother at the grocery store. She was with Larry's mother. I tried to skip the aisle, to avoid them, but they saw me and called my name. I should have walked away," she berated herself, "shouldn't have let them pull me in to their mess, but I didn't."

Swallowing, she tried to hold back her tears before continuing. "Larry's mother immediately looked at Sadie, and I could see the wheels turning in her head, David. I knew what she was thinking; she looks so much like him." The tears fell now freely. She couldn't hold them back anymore as she relived what came next. "She started calling me names, right there in the middle of the store, demanding that I hand over her grandchild. My mother was confused for a moment and then it finally clicked with her too. I ran out of that store as fast as I could. I left the cart right there in the middle of the cereal aisle."

David moved his coffee out of the way and reached across the table, covering her hand with his. "Tell me what else happened."

"Everything else was such a blur. About a week later, Larry showed up, demanding that I do a DNA test and that he was going to sue me for custody. I refused and contacted a few lawyers, but I couldn't afford any of them right away. Then my mother tried to pick Sadie up from daycare and threw a huge fit when she found out she wasn't on the list. I told everyone who would listen that you were the father. That there was no way it could be anyone else. I refused all paternity test requests from them."

Standing, she started pacing, needing to do something as she talked. "Then I messed up even more. I got a call from my mother begging me to just come for dinner and settle things. She wanted to see her grandchild for once and was willing to let everything else go. I wanted it to be done so badly that I fell for it. I'm so stupid."

"You're not stupid, Chloe."

She ignored that. He didn't know what she'd let happen. "Sadie and I get there, and dinner actually goes well. It was not dramatic; she was playing with Chloe. Time got away from us and she offered for us to stay. I accepted. I knew better, but I was so tired. Next thing I knew, she was moving us in. She was still playing the part of doting grandmother and loving mother. I thought, maybe she's changed, missed me or something."

"Oh, Chloe," David said.

"She didn't miss me. Last week, she greeted me with divorce papers and asked me to sign them, severing our marriage. I refused, told her I talked to you all the time and we'd be moving with you soon. It was the same thing I said all the time, but she wasn't buying it. Somehow my phone stopped working. I don't know what she did, and then she changed all the internet passwords, cutting me off from everything. She stopped doting on Chloe and upped her demands that I do a paternity test. Three nights ago, I woke up to Larry in my bedroom standing over me and Sadie. I screamed the house down, but no one came."

David stood then and came to her, wrapping her in his arms. She sobbed into his shirt as they stood there in the kitchen.

"Sadie woke up when I screamed and started screaming too. When she wouldn't stop, he yelled at her. He pulled his arm back to slap her and I blocked him. He had some names for me, and then he left. I haven't slept since and I didn't know I'd be able to get away."

"How did you get away?" he asked, stroking his hand up and down her back as they continued to stand there.

"I found my keys; she was never creative at hiding things. Then I just prayed it would start when I got in it. We snuck out at about three o'clock this morning and mostly drove straight here. I had to stop and get a prepaid phone so I could use a map app, and we got some food once."

"My Chloe, what have you gotten yourself into?" he asked.

"I'm sorry to show up unannounced. I hope I'm not interrupting anything."

She felt his chest jump as he chuckled. "There are no girlfriends or anything. You are always welcome here. Get some rest, Chloe. We can discuss what to do when you wake up."

"Don't let me sleep long, okay? But I'm just so tired." She pulled away, wishing she was stronger, that she could handle this and stand up to them, but she was just so tired.

"Sleep as long as you need; no one will bother you here, and you need it." He kissed her forehead and slid one hand over her hair. "Do you have any other bags that need to come inside?"

Chloe shook her head. "I was too scared to pack anything."

"Understood. Go get some rest."

"Thank you, David."

She found her way back to the bedroom and cuddled up next to Sadie. She'd sleep for an hour, max, and then she'd be refreshed enough to take on the day, she told herself. She knew though, as her eyes drifted closed, that she'd sleep forever with the scent of David on the pillow filling her senses and the knowledge that they were safe, for now.

3

———————

*D*avid waited until he hadn't heard movement for a few minutes before checking on them. He found both of them curled up on his bed sleeping. She still hadn't pulled the covers down, so he gently laid a blanket over them both.

He quietly backed out of the room and headed back downstairs to make a few calls. First, though, he needed to move her car. She'd laid her keys on top of the diaper bag, and he grabbed them before opening the garage.

There was more to this story, he thought, as he pulled her car in the garage next to his. Looking through the car quickly, he grabbed anything he thought they might need and pulled the car seat out just in case.

For extra security, he threw a car tarp over it as well. That way, if anyone was nosy enough to look in the garage, they still wouldn't see it. It wasn't the perfect solution, but it would work for now.

Satisfied that he'd done all he could, he called Mike.

"Hey man, I'm not gonna make it this morning."

"Kristin is gonna be pissed."

"Kristin doesn't have it in her to be pissed, unless you're rubbing off on her?" David joked.

"Maybe she won't be, but she will be disappointed."

"I know. Tell her I will make it up to her."

"What's going on?"

He noticed the change in Mike's voice, dropped low to indicate he didn't want anyone to hear him ask that.

"You wouldn't even believe me." David debated answering but opted for keeping it quiet for now. "I will tell you soon."

"Take care of yourself."

"Same to you."

Both men hung up, and David set about taking stock of his kitchen. He hadn't been home in a while, so to say it was lacking a few things was putting it mildly. He pulled out a notepad and made a small list of groceries to get started. He would ask what else Chloe and Sadie needed when she got up.

"Hello," a small voice said from behind him.

"Hi," he answered back, turning to face the little girl.

"Momma said you're gonna keep the bad man away," she told him matter-of-factly.

"I am going to do my best," he confirmed.

She titled her head to one side and looked at him. "I like you then."

David chuckled; she was an honest little girl. He stood, realizing he had no toys or anything and hadn't seen any in the car. Sadie just stood there looking at him.

"Do you want to watch TV?" he asked.\

"Momma's sleeping," she cautioned.

"We won't turn it up loud, okay?"

She nodded and held out her hand for David to take. He stood and took the small hand in his, walking her to the living room.

It took her a while to find something she wanted to watch, flipping through almost everything on his streaming service before going back to one of the first things she'd looked at. Now she was comfortably sitting on the couch, engrossed in her show.

David checked his phone, knowing she'd be hungry soon. "Hey Sadie, I'm going to go check on your mom, okay?"

Sadie nodded again, not looking at him.

"Stay here," he told her for good measure before double-checking the locks and heading upstairs.

Chloe was still sleeping in the bed when he went upstairs. She hadn't moved except to curl up tighter into a ball. He took in the sight before waking her, a sight that he believed he'd never see: Chloe peacefully sleeping in his bed.

Gently, he brought his hand to her hair and stroked it as he said her name, trying to wake her up easily. Rather than wake, she moaned and turned into his touch.

"Chloe," he said louder this time with a throaty voice.

"Hmm?" she said, still not awake.

"Chloe, baby, it's time to wake up," he said, fighting his own urge to crawl into the bed next to her and hold her tight.

Her eyes popped open as she jerked herself upright. "Oh my gosh, how late is it?" she said in a panic.

"Not very late, just about lunchtime," he answered and stepped away from the bed.

"Where's Sadie?" she asked, scooting out of the bed to stand, ready to run for her daughter.

"Calm down; she's just watching TV. Couldn't take her eyes away from it when I left her." He smiled.

"I'm sorry, she should have woken me up. I didn't mean for you to babysit." Running fingers through her hair, she stretched and straightened.

Her comment hurt, like a splash of cold water on his fantasy. Sadie wasn't his and neither was Chloe. He needed to remember that.

"I just wanted to know what to feed her. I don't have much, but is there anything she can't have?" he asked.

"Oh, no, she doesn't have any allergies or anything, just typical kid rules, not too many sweets."

They stood there in his bedroom, both of them watching the other. She looked amazing standing there, sleep still not cleared from her despite the small panic. Before he could act on his desire to pull her close and kiss her, he turned to go back downstairs.

"Come on, I'll show you what I have, and you can tell me what you need."

She didn't reply but followed him down the stairs and into the living room before going into the kitchen. He listened as she checked on Sadie. It wasn't like he was eavesdropping he told himself; he didn't need to strain to hear them.

"Sadie, girl, what are you doing up?" she asked.

"The sun is up, Momma."

He smiled at the child's honest and true answer.

"Next time wake me up too, okay?" Chloe told her.

"You said he's my daddy. Don't daddies let mommies sleep too?"

His chest tightened at Sadie's words. So she knew who he was to her, on paper at least. That was something he hadn't expected. It humbled him and had him grabbing for a chair at the table to sit before he fell down.

He missed any response that Chloe had given her. His heart was hammering as he tried to sort out his own thoughts. It answered why she had been so trusting of him this morning when she woke up.

Chloe walked into the kitchen and stopped, looking at him still sitting at the table trying to get his thoughts together. She grabbed the door frame before speaking.

"You heard," she said, her voice so soft it was almost a whisper.

He nodded, but didn't have the words to answer. It made sense that she would have told Sadie about him at some point, but he didn't think she would have told her where they were going.

"I'm—" she started before he cut her off.

"Don't say you're sorry again," he cut in. "I'm not upset, just surprised."

Slowly he stood up, making sure he had his balance before moving to the cabinets. Chloe watched him carefully but didn't move.

"On second thought, maybe I should order something, or go get us something for lunch. Like I said, I only got back in town last night."

"David." His name was like a plea on her lips. "I was going to tell you."

"Chloe, there's a lot we need to talk about but, it can wait until tonight when Sadie is in bed." He nearly said "our daughter," but he didn't mean it as a threat, and that's how she would have taken it.

"Okay," her small voice answered.

After a lot of back and forth, he convinced her to let him take them to lunch and to the grocery store to get real food. She'd insisted on cooking dinner tonight, something he wasn't going to argue with. If she wanted to cook, it was fine by him.

However, he saw her in the store, counting the cost of each item she put in the basket. He didn't need her to do that. Instead, every time she debated something and put it back, he picked it up and put it in the cart.

She'd fussed at him, saying it wasn't needed, but it wasn't always about need; sometimes you needed to have your wants filled too. As they loaded the groceries into his truck, he finally worked up the nerve to ask her his burning question.

"How long do you plan on staying here?"

"I don't know," she said with a sigh. "I know this isn't what you signed up for all those years ago. I just didn't know where else to go."

"Look at me, Chloe." He waited for her to focus on him. "I told you 5 years ago that I would move you with me and make this a real marriage. The offer still stands."

"David, you don't want this. I'm a mess with more problems than good things."

That pissed him off in a way he hadn't even expected. "Never assume what I want, Chloe. You might find you are wrong."

He shut the tailgate on his truck and walked around to the driver's side, leaving her standing there and him feeling like an ass. He hadn't meant to snap at her, but to think he was just wanting out of this was wrong of her.

After she climbed in the truck, he gave her no choice on their next step. "Rumor has it that you two ladies need some new clothes, and maybe some toys?" he asked. It was meant for Chloe to hear, but the question was directed at Sadie.

"Yes!" she said from the backseat.

He chuckled as he drove them out of the parking lot and on their way to another store.

"The groceries," Chloe tried.

"They will be fine; it's not going to warm up much today," he said in answer. The ice cream might get a little soft, but it would be fine after a little time in the freezer.

He pulled them into a department store and hopped out. This time he didn't wait for Chloe to come and get Sadie. He opened the door and helped her out of the car seat, setting her down and taking her hand.

"Up!" she said, reaching both her arms up to him.

"Sadie, you're a big girl," her mother chided.

"It's okay for today. I don't mind." He picked her up and settled her on his hip. "But just this one. Next time, you have to listen to you mom."

He watched Chloe roll her eyes at him, but she smiled, showing she wasn't upset with him. He should have told her no because her mom had said no, but this one time, he wanted to. It wasn't like he was going to hold her long; he intended to spoil them both, and he had a feeling she was going to want to run around and pick things out.

4

———————

Chloe took the tags off an overwhelming amount of clothes as she put them in the washer. David had gone overboard and bought them too much stuff, but considering they didn't bring anything with them, she didn't argue at first.

Then he'd bought nearly the whole toy aisle and was currently upstairs putting a spare bedroom into a little girl's dream room. She didn't want this; it was so good for them, too good. What would happen when they left? Sadie was going to be too attached to David.

At this point, Chloe was going to be too attached to David. She'd had fun today though. Once she'd given in to David's need to buy them things, she'd let go and even grabbed a few things she didn't really need.

She'd grown up with wealth and designer clothes, and until she'd gotten pregnant, she'd never had to worry about money. Once she'd moved out and really truly learned the value of money, she found she didn't even mind shopping at box stores and department stores. It was freeing to just pick something she liked with no concern of what someone might say about it or who might already have it.

"Momma!" Sadie yelled. "Come see my room."

Chloe groaned. Her daughter was attached already. If only her mom could keep herself from doing the same.

"In a minute. I'm washing our clothes," she answered.

"Hurry!" Sadie said frantically, as though her pretty room might suddenly disappear.

She shook her head and returned to the task at hand and her thoughts. David was a great guy—the best really. He'd saved her once before, and she felt awful that she was here again looking for more help.

He would help her, he always would, she knew that. She just didn't want to pressure him into a full-on marriage that he never asked for in the first place. She also had to talk herself down from wanting it to be real. Every time he mentioned it, she found herself wanting it more and more.

David had been her best friend in high school until they graduated. He'd gone on to the military, and she'd stayed behind. Eventually, they'd lost touch, though it had been more her fault than his. She would get busy and forget to reply, and then it would go too long and she couldn't reply.

She'd liked him back then and even wanted to be more than friends, but she was scared to move forward with that because if it ruined the friendship, she wouldn't have a true friend anymore. Most of the friends she'd had then were fake. They were her friends because they were supposed to be since they were all from money.

Looking back on her life before and after Sadie, she preferred the new one. It was hard having Sadie on her own, but she learned valuable lessons about her life that she wouldn't have before.

Finished with the laundry, she made her way to what was now Sadie's room. The pink hit her eyes and pulled them everywhere.

In the middle of one wall was a big bed, probably a queen, and David had hung a pink canopy over it with fairy lights on it. Her two new stuffed animals sat in the middle of the pink bedspread. She hadn't had a chance to look at everything before Sadie pulled her all the way in.

David stood by the closet, grinning like a fool. He was so proud of himself that even though she wanted to complain he'd done too much, she couldn't burst his bubble. Toys were scattered and the few books that Chloe had made her get were stacked on the dresser.

Sadie spun in a circle with her arms out. "Do you like it, Momma?" she asked.

Chloe bit her lip as she nodded, fighting back tears at the happiness her daughter was exuding. "I love it," she told her, crouching down and opening her arms for a hug.

How many times had Chloe wished she could give all this to her? So many. She had the money from David, but it felt like she was using him whenever she spent it, so she only used it for emergencies—once to pay the rest of her rent when she'd been too sick to work, and that was about it.

"I know I overdid it, but she loves it," David whispered as Sadie went back to playing with one of her new dolls.

His breath on her neck as he whispered sent goosebumps down her body. She only barely held back the shiver that was coming along with it.

"David, we need to talk," she told him.

"I agree," he confirmed.

A doorbell stopped any further conversation from happening. She panicked and grabbed Sadie's hand.

"Let me go see who it is," David told her, leaving them both in the room and pulling the door almost closed behind him.

She stood by the door and put one finger over her lips to tell Sadie to be quiet. She looked scared and Chloe felt a knife stab at her heart that her daughter was going through this because of her.

A woman's happy voice could be heard now, but she couldn't make out what was being said. David had invited her in though because the voice was louder than it would have been outside. Jealousy that she had no right to feel crawled up now.

Walking away from the door, she told Chloe to stay quiet, but she sat down to play dolls with her. She had no sooner done that than David appeared in the room.

"It's just friends. You two come down and meet them." He held out his hand to help Chloe off the floor.

She took it without a word. When she was up, he didn't let go, stroking her knuckles with his thumb.

"It's okay," he assured her.

He let go and picked up Sadie and her doll to bring them downstairs with Chloe right behind them. She let a hand go to her hair and quickly undid the ponytail before smoothing it back up again.

"What's going on?" a male voice greeted them as they walked down the stairs. A woman was with him.

"Mike, this is Chloe," he pulled her from behind him and put an arm around her, drawing her into his side, "my wife, and my daughter, Sadie."

Like something out of a cartoon, the visitors' mouths fell open. She half-expected someone to pull a cord and wind them back up.

"My question stands," Mike said.

David set Sadie down. "Can you say hi to everyone?" he asked her.

"Hi," Sadie said quietly and hugged David's leg.

David crouched down to her level. "All is well, okay? You can go play toys some more if you want, okay?"

"Bye." Sadie waved behind her as she took off back up the stairs.

"Hi Chloe, I'm Kristin. This fool is my husband, Mike. Manners aren't his forte right now." Kirstin held out her hand for Chloe to shake.

"It's okay. Nice to meet you." She shook Kristin's hand. David never let her go from his side.

"What made you drop by?" David asked, avoiding the question from Mike.

"We have news for you, but it appears you have news for us. When did this happen?" Mike pressed.

"Five years ago next month," David answered.

"Nope. No way you've been married that long and we didn't know," Kristin said.

"Hate to break it to you." David smiled.

"I need explanations," Mike said gruffly.

"You first," David countered.

"Oh hell, are we really doing testosterone wars right now?" Kirstin put her hands on her hips and stared down both men that towered over her. "We're having a baby!" she announced and rubbed her stomach.

For the first time since they came downstairs, David let go of Chloe. He scooped Kristin into a hug and spun her around. "Congratulations!" he said as he set her down and patted Mike on the back. "What did Daniel say?"

"He's excited, in his way," Kristin answered.

"Cranky?"

"Does he have another mood?" she laughed.

"You got our news, so what's yours?" Mike asked.

"It's a bit of a long story. Have a seat." David told them everything as Chloe sat quietly by his side.

Shocked that he was saying anything, she couldn't have added anything to it if she wanted. If she thought she was shocked that he was telling them, she was utterly floored by their reaction.

When he finished talking, Mike and Kristin looked at each other and burst out laughing.

"I'm sorry, the reason you're here isn't funny. We aren't laughing at you," Kristin tried to assure her, while still laughing and wiping tears.

David turned to her. "They had a fake marriage, and so did her brother, my friend."

"Not true," Mike told him. "We had a fake engagement; the marriage is real."

"Whatever."

Chloe sat there stunned. She wanted to laugh at the absurdity of it all, but at the same time, she was overwhelmed with the whole situation that was her life. What she wanted to do was cry.

"So, what are you guys gonna do?" Kristin asked.

"We are going to talk tonight and determine what we should do," David told her as though the woman had every right to know.

"Let me call a few friends and see what I can find out. Can you send me the names?" Mike asked.

David nodded and leaned closer to Chloe as he shifted to get his phone out of his pocket. He quickly shot a message off and then set the phone on the coffee table.

Chloe was overwhelmed and sat in silence watching everything. While David and Mike talked, Kristin sometimes joined but sometimes Chloe would catch Kristin looking at her.

"David," Kristin said, "I think Chloe and I are going to go talk."

He nodded and didn't look up. Kristin left the living room after that. It took Chloe a minute for her brain to register that she was supposed to follow.

"Have a seat," Kristin told her, gesturing to a chair. "You look terrified; just sit here and gather your thoughts."

That broke the dam that had been holding the tears back since arriving at David's house. She'd pushed them back then, but this little kindness did her in.

Chloe fell into the chair and put her head down into her hands. Kristin was out of the seat in a second and wrapping Chloe in a hug.

"It's okay," she crooned, soothing Chloe as the tears fell.

"I'm sorry," Chloe told her and tried to pull away.

"For what? Being exhausted and scared? Nope, nothing to apologize for." Kristin stepped away and went back to her chair. Cry if you need to. I'll be here either way."

"Thank you." She grabbed a napkin off the table and blotted her face. "I hate crying."

"No one likes it, but you usually feel better afterwards."

Chloe nodded; she did feel a little better. "I just don't know what I am going to do," she confessed.

"David will help you," Kristin told her, but she was watching and Chloe knew she was trying to determine if Chloe was going to hurt him.

"He will," she agreed. "I hate that I had to come here though, for his sake."

"That little girl thinks David is her dad?"

Chloe nodded.

"Then let him be. He wouldn't' hurt either of you, and he's always wanted a family. He's never admitted anything, but you can tell in the way he looks at other people, with a longing. I didn't know he was married, but that makes sense now."

"I don't think he really wants me. Sadie sure, he loved her instantly, but that doesn't mean he needs to stay married to me. It feels like trapping him."

"Are you trapping him?" Kristin asked directly.

"No, of course not!" Chloe adamantly denied.

"Then what is there to worry about? Maybe ask him what he wants."

"Maybe..." Chloe let the conversation drift off as she contemplated how tonight's conversation was going to go.

5

———————

Kristin and Mike hung out for about an hour at David's before they left. David and Mike had come up with a good plan to do some digging into both families to determine why they would want to push this issue now.

Mike had contacts that could discreetly gather information without David needing to get his work involved. He would go to his bosses for help, but if he could get the information without them, he would prefer the more discreet route.

"Your friends are really nice," Chloe told him.

"Mike and Daniel served with me, and we have always been there for each other. They will help us get through this."

She went upstairs and checked on Sadie while David waited for her to come back. He really wanted a chance to talk to her and to let her know he was going to take care of everything for both of them. He was going to ask her to stay.

"She still playing?" David asked.

"She fell asleep actually, with her dolls in that big bed."

David laughed. "Wore her out, huh?"

"I'm going to make dinner," Chloe told him and headed for the kitchen.

"I can help. Plus, we can talk now that she's asleep."

If he hadn't been truly watching her, he wouldn't have seen the small misstep that she made, the only indication that she had heard him.

"Chloe," he said, reaching for her hand. "It's going to be okay. Let me help you both. Stay with me." Pouring all of it into one rushed moment, he pulled her to him.

"I can't David. This isn't what you want. You'll realize that one day." She put a hand to his chest to push him away.

David took a step back without any more prompting. It was never his intention to make her feel trapped.

"Stop assuming what I want," David said through gritted teeth.

"I can take care of dinner," Chloe said, and he knew she was dismissing him.

"We are going to have to talk at some point," he told her.

"You're right, but it doesn't have to be now."

"Soon," he promised and left her to the kitchen.

He went back to the living room and took a seat to think on the possibilities of what was happening. He wanted Chloe to stay here, to make a family with her, but clearly she wasn't wanting to.

The hardest thing for him to do after everything was settled would be to let Chloe and Sadie walk out of his life. He didn't want to force her into any decisions—that went against everything he stood for.

However, that didn't mean he wasn't going to try to convince her this was right. He loved Sadie already. She was a sweet kid, and her mom had clearly raised her well so far. Her mom, he smiled, had always had a hold on him well before the marriage.

She'd been one of his few friends back home, and they'd done a lot together before he'd gone into the military. Then she'd written some but had slowly stopped until they'd no longer been in touch at all.

Mike had his friends looking into things, the same ones that David could call too, but maybe more eyes wouldn't hurt. He opened his phone and sent off a quick email to a private investigator that he'd meet on his security job asking for a call.

Before he could put his phone down, it rang. Daniel wasn't someone who called anyone often so seeing his number pop up had David groaning before answering.

"Hey Daniel," he answered.

"You're freaking married?" he asked.

"Yep." David let it hang and waited for Daniel to reply.

"That's it? Yep? What is going on?" He was practically yelling through the phone.

"I'm not sure yet," David answered honestly. "I'm sure Mike filled you in on everything so I am not sure what you're hoping to hear from me."

"Don't let her take advantage of you," Daniel cautioned. Having been through a very difficult injury and horrible former fiancée, Daniel knew about women taking advantage.

"She's not."

"How can you know?" Daniel's voice had lowered, but the cynicism was there still.

"She's got nothing to get from me." It was that simple. Other than some protection from this situation, there was nothing for her to gain, especially as she fought against making this marriage real.

"Money?" Daniel asked bluntly.

"I've been sending her money for years. She's rarely used it." He sighed and pushed a hand through his hair. "There's thousands in that account."

"Hmm," Daniel said noncommittally.

"I want this to be real, Daniel. She doesn't."

"Shit," was the only response he got and the call went silent.

"David," he heard Macy, Daniel's wife say. "Bring her by soon?"

"I will," he promised. He absolutely intended to bring her to meet his friends, so she could see the kind of friends she could have too—the kind of support that comes with letting people in your life, the right kind of people.

"Let us know when you want to get together. We can meet at the diner or something if you want instead of here."

"I will."

He hung up and thought on her suggestion. Meeting at the diner might not be a bad idea. She could see how great everyone was and how supportive. It would be good for Sadie to meet some other people as well, including Macy's brother, who was older, but would definitely play with her.

Smiling, he wandered back into the kitchen to run the idea past Chloe. He paused at the entry as he watched her humming and dancing while she cooked. This was a sight he could get used to.

Her hair swayed in its ponytail as she moved her hips. She was curvy, probably from having Sadie, he mused, as she'd had some curves before but had definitely filled them in a bit over the years. Her jeans and simple t-shirt did nothing to enhance her curves or show them off, and somehow the fact that she wasn't trying made her even sexier to him.

Before he'd married her, and even when he did, for that matter, she'd never not had makeup on. She was always completely put together. That was likely her mother's doing, and he was happy to see that hadn't been something she held on to.

If she wanted to wear makeup, that was great and her choice, but if she didn't want to, he liked her natural beauty. Her green eyes contrasted with her hair all on their own. He face had rounded some over the years but was still pixie-like.

She stopped humming and tasted what she had on the stove. Adding some more seasonings, she went back to stirring and started a new song.

Recognizing the song, David waited until he knew the next part and came up behind her, spinning her into a dance as he sang along. She was surprised at first, but then laughed and allowed him to lead her around the kitchen as they both sang the song.

Sooner than he liked, the song ended and Chloe stepped out of his arms and went back to the stove.

"I was thinking of taking you two to dinner with my friends one day this week," he began. "Would that be okay?"

"David —"

The doorbell rang again, interrupting them.

"I'm going to disable that damn thing," he muttered as he went to answer it.

Chloe grabbed his arm before they made it to the door. "That's my mother's car," she whispered.

David stopped and looked at her. She was chewing her bottom lip and her hand was tightly gripped onto his arm. The fact that she'd initiated contact with him told him what he needed to know.

There was no hiding though, he thought, as the doorbell rang again. He'd hidden the car, but it would be obvious that Chloe and Sadie had come here. His stomach sank as he wondered what would have happened if he hadn't been here.

"We face this head on. There is nothing she can do." David leaned over and placed a kiss on her forehead.

"I...are you sure?" she asked.

"You can do this," he reassured her. Taking her hand from his arm, he placed it in his other hand. "I'm right here, we can do this."

He led her to the door and waited as she took a steadying breath before he opened it wide so they could both be seen.

"Chloe!" her mother screeched. "What are you doing?"

David went to speak, but Chloe squeezed his hand and spoke instead.

"Making dinner for my husband and daughter," she answered simply. The grip on his hand belayed her fear, but overall she was calm and had managed to deliver that statement with just the right amount of boredom and innocence.

"That is not what I mean." He mother stomped her foot and gestured with her hand towards the house. "Aren't you going to invite me in?"

"No," David answered.

"That's not very hospitable, and I wasn't talking to you," she scolded, adjusting her black blazer and touching the pearls at her neck. "Chloe, I have been looking for you. You just snuck out and disappeared."

"Was there something you needed, aside from letting Larry in the house and into my room?" Chloe asked.

"You know very well you cannot keep his child from him." She wasn't denying she had done that and she wasn't making excuses; it was fact to her. She moved her hands with every word she spoke, causing her perfect little bob to bounce her white hair as she did.

"Sadie is my child," David corrected.

"We all know that's not true," she laughed.

"My name is on her birth certificate; she is my child."

David couldn't cross his arms like he wanted to without letting go of Chloe, so he chose the next best intimidation move here and stepped out onto the porch, closing the door behind them. Stepping into her space had her backing up and wobbling a little as she nearly fell off the porch.

"If you were just looking for Chloe, you have found her. Now, we are asking you to leave," David said with much more calm that he felt.

"You can't make me leave; she's my child." The irony here wasn't lost on him or Chloe who rolled her eyes.

"She's my wife and that trumps you. However, she is an adult regardless and wants you to leave." He was letting his voice slowly get louder, but he wasn't yelling, yet.

"You were always a rude boy with no manners." She wagged her finger at him.

David smiled in response. He didn't care what she had thought of him years ago. She was just lucky right now that he didn't tell her what he thought of her.

"Mother, I am cooking and need to get back to it, please excuse us."

Turning her back to her mother, she went on her tiptoes and kissed David on the cheek before opening the door. David followed her in and shut the door again, turning the lock with a satisfying click.

"Go check on the food. She isn't going to come in," he told her.

Chloe looked in his eyes and held him there for just a moment before she walked off. David stood by the door and waited for her to get in her car and drive off before he went to check on Chloe again.

"Chloe, we need to talk now," he told her as he came up behind her.

She leaned back into him for a breath and then shut the stove off. "You're right."

They both sat at the table but while David looked at Chloe, she looked at the table, not making eye contact with him.

"Look, I know where you stand, but I want to make it clear where I stand. I want to make this real, regardless of your hesitations on believing me."

"We have a lot of crap in our lives."

"We all do," he tried.

"It's not the same, and you know it."

"Maybe not, but that doesn't change how I feel. I wanted to make it real in the beginning. I told you that then."

"And just raise someone else's child? Take in some pregnant chick you used to know and make it work forever?" She let out a sad sigh. "It wouldn't have worked. And what you see now are good days by comparison. Wait until Sadie throws a fit about needing to leave, or refuses dinner, and it stops being the picture perfect moment."

"I know you believe what you are saying, but I want it all, Chloe, the good, the bad, all of it. All I can do is show you that I will be here for you."

6

———

ast night, Sadie had interrupted them before dinner, but they'd finally gotten to talk again after she'd gone to bed for the night. She'd agreed that faking it would be the best way to proceed for now.

David had also mentioned calling a lawyer, to which she had agreed was the best thing to do. She didn't like that he'd hired a private investigator but didn't argue that either. If they were lucky, they could find out why it was so important that Sadie was Larry's, and if they had that information, then possibly they could stop him from trying to force this.

As to her mother, she hadn't come back. She would, of course, but for now, she was gone. It would likely be a day or two before she showed up with a new tactic. Thankfully, Sadie had slept through the events.

Her mother had chased her much faster than expected. She really thought a few days would go by before she would show up. David had been her support for handling her mother and she'd needed it. Being able to tell her to leave was the biggest win she'd had in forever.

Last night, he'd also refused to let Chloe sleep in the other spare room. He insisted that his bed was more comfortable and that was where she should sleep. After arguing with him for way too long, she gave in and let him sleep in the spare room.

He'd gotten up earlier than her, and was making pancakes with Sadie when she came down. David had Sadie standing on a chair in the kitchen and stirring the mix. The kitchen was a complete disaster.

Chloe was torn when she saw them. Clearly he was embracing having a daughter, and she knew with every passing minute it would be harder and harder for Sadie to leave. She couldn't shake the feeling that not leaving was trapping David though.

"Momma, I'm cooking!" Sadie waved her spoon slinging mix on the floor and on David's shirt.

Grinning, David took the spoon. "There won't be anything left to cook if you keep doing that," he gently teased her and put the spoon back in the bowl before looking at Chloe. "She's going to need a shower."

"I can see that. Did you two use every pan you own?" Chloe laughed as she stepped into the kitchen all the way.

"Maybe." David's grin turned sheepish.

"I will start cleaning then as you two cook us some pancakes."

"We can clean it," David told her.

"No, no. You cook, I'll clean. Also this is stressing me out a little bit."

"Sorry." David's smile fell.

"I'm not upset. It smells like they will be delicious, and I don't mind doing the dishes." She hadn't meant to take the joy out of his morning.

"We folded laundry first," David told her as he moved Sadie's stool from the counter to the stove.

"Thanks." She had forgotten there was more laundry going.

"Alright, kiddo. Let's get cooking."

She cleaned the kitchen as they cooked and then they all sat down to eat breakfast together. The pancakes were delicious, made with happiness for sure. She had always believed you could taste the mood of the cook in their food.

After breakfast, she took Sadie to get cleaned up as David finished cleaning the kitchen.

"Momma?" Sadie asked once she was clean and dressed.

"What's up?"

"Can I call him Daddy like other people call their daddies?"

Oh, she was done for, was all she could think. "Umm, that's up to David."

"Okay!" Sadie took off out of the room with Chloe trying to catch her.

She hadn't meant that to be the end of the conversation, but much to her dismay, it had been.

"Hey!" Sadie yelled as she hit the bottom of the stairs.

Chloe nearly fell down them trying to keep up. She had just made it to the kitchen when Sadie asked David her question.

"That's okay with me if it's okay with your momma?" David looked up with the question in his eyes.

There was so much in his eyes just then. The question, the hope, the need. There was no reason to say no, but still she hesitated.

"It's okay," he said looking at Chloe.

Tears sprang to her eyes as she looked at these two and the light that had quickly disappeared in David's eyes when she hadn't answered right away.

"Of course it's okay," she told him, pasting a smile on her face that she hoped was more cheerful than she felt. "I was just out of breath from chasing her down the stairs."

He didn't believe her, not one bit, and the eyebrow he raised showed her that.

"Yay!" Sadie yelled again.

"Sadie. Stop yelling," Chloe scolded.

"I can't, I'm too happy-full," Sadie yelled again.

"Happy-full?" David asked.

"It means she's full of happy." Chloe shrugged. Sadie had made that up a while ago.

"I am happy-full too, Sadie," he told her, picking her up for a hug.

"You still shouldn't yell though," he told her but tickled her side as he did.

"I want to go play now," she said and wiggled out of David's arms as he set her down.

With the same force she ran into the kitchen with, she left the adults there to deal with the aftermath of an innocent child's questions.

"I'm sorry she asked that," David started. "I swear I didn't say anything to her this morning to make her ask."

"I didn't think you did for a second. She knows who you are to her, so it made sense that she was going to ask. I should have been prepared for it." She really should have seen in coming.

"Still, you didn't want her to."

"It's not that, not really. It's just, what happens when we leave, David?" She fidgeted with the hem of her t-shirt.

"What happens if you don't?" he answered. "She's a great kid, you know? I won't hurt her. I wish you would give me a chance."

"It's not about you not being a good person or anything like that," Chloe pleaded with him to listen to her. "I don't want you to feel trapped with this. I don't want you to feel stuck with us because of a decision years ago." On a whisper, she added, "I don't want you to regret this."

Coming here had been a mistake. It was sheer impulse that she'd driven to his house. While she'd planned to leave, she hadn't considered where she was going. Deep down she knew where she was going, but she didn't really think about it until she got here, and he hadn't answered the door.

With Sadie asleep in the backseat, she'd let the tears fall at her impulsive decision when she'd gotten back in the car. She hadn't been that impulsive in years, and she'd pinned all of her hopes on David and had no backup plan.

In the last day, she'd learned that David said he wanted more but was scared to believe it. Her life was a mess and she was wrong for bringing him into it, again. She should have divorced him years ago and given him his freedom back.

It had been selfish of her to stay married. It definitely wasn't financially motivated, but it made her feel more secure to say she was married. Often though she didn't think about being married, unless she was asked, which happened sometimes.

The tough thing was that every time she saw him with Sadie, she wanted it to be real too. He was so good with her, and Sadie loved him already with all the innocence of a child who doesn't know the real world situations they are in.

Slowly, David approached her as she came out of her musings. She watched him, and while part of her wanted to flee, the other part of her won—the part that couldn't move at all.

"What will it take to get you to understand that I want you?" he asked.

She didn't get to answer, didn't have one anyway. David's hand came to back of her neck at the same time as his lips crushed down on hers. It wasn't a gentle kiss; it was demanding and intense.

His tongue urged her lips open and she complied, giving in to the man before her. The man who was through pleading with words for now and had moved on to showing her what he wanted. The kiss deepened as she backed into the wall behind her and David's other hand came up to her cheek.

David broke the kiss and took a step back. She watched as his chest rose and fell rapidly, letting her know he was just as out of breath as she was.

"I. Want. You." He spoke each word as its own sentence before turning and leaving the kitchen.

It took Chloe a few minutes to steady herself before she could leave the wall. She brought shaky fingers to her lips. This was unexpected, but whether it was good or bad remained to be seen. Now she had more thoughts to wrap her head around. On a sigh, she went in search of Sadie.

7

Kissing Chloe in the kitchen yesterday hadn't been his intention. He'd wanted to, for a long time, but he hadn't meant to do it out of frustration.

The kiss though, it had left him weak. He'd barely managed to stop it and step away, and it had taken him what felt like an hour to even settle his breathing and racing heart. Chloe hadn't pushed him away though and that made him smile.

If she thought she could push him out of her life now, she was mistaken. He wasn't going to make her, but he was damn sure going to try to convince her that they were what he wanted and that she needed to stay.

He'd arranged for Mike and Daniel and their wives to meet them all for dinner tonight at the diner. It was a bit of a drive, so they were doing an early dinner to keep from having to drive home too late with Sadie. Plus, the forecast called for storms later.

A ping from his phone let him know he had and email. He opened his phone, seeing an email from the private investigator that he'd hired.

Skimming through it once, he went in search of Chloe and his computer before reading it fully.

"Hey, we have an update," he told her when he found her.

She was sitting on the couch on her own computer, looking at a college from what he could see, before she snapped it shut. He filed that knowledge away for later.

"What does it say?" she asked, scooting over on the couch for him to sit down.

He opened his laptop and pulled up his email so they could both look. He read it in full this time, keeping one eye on Chloe.

"Is this real?" she asked.

"He has no reason to lie," David said.

The email had said that Larry had gotten into an accident three years ago that had left him sterile. While normally this wouldn't have affected Chloe or anyone else, his father's will specifically stated that if he wanted to inherit the massive amount of money that was left to him, he needed to get married and have a child.

The details were direct but the email also stated that they were working to get a copy of the will to determine the exact language.

Chloe put a hand over her mouth as she read it again from David's computer. "He's not going to let this go," she said. "He won't let the money go."

"Come here." David set the laptop down on the table to put his arms around Chloe, pulling her to him.

He felt her body shake as she cried. His shirt was growing damp, and the position he'd hugged her in was awkward to hold, but he'd stay like that as long as she needed.

"It's going to be okay," he soothed and ran his hand up and down her back. "We will figure this out."

"I'm sorry." She pulled back and wiped her cheeks. "Your shirt."

"My shirt is yours whenever you need it, and the shoulder underneath. We will get through this, you'll see." He believed it too. There was no way he was going to let anyone take Sadie from her, or him.

He picked the laptop up again and forward the email out to Daniel and Mike before replying to thank for the update and ask when they might have a copy of the will. He didn't know how they were going to get it, but he didn't dare ask. He needed answers.

He heard Sadie coming down the stairs. "Go get cleaned up, I've got her."

Meeting Sadie at the steps, he picked her up and carried her to the kitchen to search for lunch. By the time Chloe came down again, looking better than she had when she was on the couch, he had Sadie at the table with lunch, quietly eating.

David walked to her and hugged her again. "It will be okay," he assured her.

Chloe gave into the hug for just a second before stepping back. "I'll start crying again," she whispered and went to Sadie instead.

Grabbing another plate from the counter, he set Chloe's sandwich in front of her and joined them. They let Sadie lead the conversation with occasional reminders from Chloe not to talk with her mouth full.

After lunch, they watched a movie and then got ready for dinner. Chloe had changed outfits three times that he was aware of, and Sadie had picked out a dress he had bought her the other day.

"Come on, Chloe, we need to head out."

"I think I'm ready," she said as she came down the stairs. "I don't know. I didn't bring any makeup and my hair is being a pain." She looked sad, and he couldn't resist touching her.

She was wearing jeans that fit her perfectly and a green sweater that brought out her eyes even more. Her wavy hair was doing its own thing as usual, but he liked it like that.

He put a hand on her chin and tipped her head to look at him. "You look great, amazing. You don't need makeup either. It's casual as can be, so this is perfect."

She smiled but he could tell she didn't really believe him. "I look a mess."

"You look great," he argued.

"I'm not fishing for compliments," she told him.

"I never thought you were."

With a glance over his shoulder to make sure Sadie was occupied, he leaned down and pressed a kiss to her lips. She sighed, and he felt her relax just a bit.

"Let's go." He released her chin and picked up her coat, helping her slip into it and then Sadie's next.

Everyone was ready and they piled into his truck, Sadie in the backseat and Chloe next to him in the front. He handed Sadie his phone and headphones. He had pulled up some kid shows for the ride.

"You don't have to do that; she will be fine," Chloe told him as they buckled themselves in.

"I know I don't have to, but it's a long ride and I want her to be comfortable," he said.

"You're spoiling her," Chloe said.

She rolled her eyes as he grinned. "Pick some music," he told her and they started the drive.

He was smiling as they hit the interstate. Her taste in music hadn't changed, and he enjoyed listening to her sing along to the country music playing through his speakers.

His hand had been on her knee for most of the ride, and other than look at him questioningly once he did it, she hadn't remarked on it. She also hadn't asked him to move it or moved away. It was a win by any measure.

"What was the school stuff you were looking at on the computer earlier?" David asked.

"Oh, umm, I was just starting to go back to school when this happened, and I was looking at when the next semester would start to see if I can swing it." Biting her bottom lip again, she looked out the window.

"What were you going to school for?" he asked.

"Interior design, maybe. I'm not sure it's practical though."

"Why not?"

"I don't know if there's enough demand for it, and I need a good paying job to support Sadie. At this point, I just need a job." He barely heard her last sentence.

"Will you not have a job if you go back?"

Chloe shook her head. "We were all on notice not to miss any days, and I've missed more than my vacation would cover."

"I'm sorry."

His thoughts swirled the rest of the drive. If she chose to stay with him, she wouldn't need to work and could continue her schooling. He didn't need her income to support them.

It was something he would bring up later though. He didn't want to get into that debate again right now about her staying. Tonight he wanted her to relax and make friends.

He liked Macy and Kristin enough, and he really hoped they got along with Chloe. It would make things easier for sure if everyone got along well. It would also give Chloe someone to talk to, something that he knew she needed.

As they pulled up, David got out and walked around to Chloe, helping her out before taking his phone from Sadie and helping her out as well. Walking in, he took in the booths that lined the windows and led Chloe and Sadie to the tables in the back.

"David!" Marge, the owner of the diner, greeted him. "Long time, no see. Back in town?" she asked.

Marge was a thin older woman who enjoyed working and owning the diner. She loved everyone but was a tough woman when she needed to be. He'd watched her put more than one person in their place over the years.

"Yes, ma'am," he told her.

"And who are these lovely ladies?" she asked looking at Chloe and Sadie.

"Marge, this is my wife Chloe and my daughter, Sadie."

Chloe's eyes got wide and she looked away, looking anywhere but at him or Marge.

"Well I'll be," Marge said. "I'm sure that's an interesting tale, but I don't have time to pry into tonight. The Pillars will be in shortly, you've been warned. It was nice meeting you both. Make this man happy, he deserves it," she said before leaving them at their table.

"Who are the Pillars?" Chloe asked.

David just laughed in response. She had no idea the force of nature those three ladies could be. At this point, they should be grateful they were already married and no bachelorette party was going to be forced on her. He'd heard about the strippers at Kristin's and how the Pillars had enjoyed themselves more than everyone else. He shuddered at the image that thought provoked.

8

———————

*C*hloe had been confident at one point in her life. It wasn't now, but somewhere deep down, she knew she how to act around strangers even when she was nervous, but it was very deep and she couldn't find it.

David had introduced them as his wife and daughter to dozens of people already tonight and it was early. Mike and Kristin had only just arrived, and the other couple they were meeting were running behind. They had a new baby, Kristin had told her.

It seemed everyone in this town knew David, and each one had to speak to him. The ones who didn't speak to him were getting their info from the ones who did. She watched them look their way and then discuss.

She hated it. It made her nervous and uncomfortable. Sadie, on the other hand, relished all the attention. She was adored and was living her best life with a million fans.

"It's okay," Kristin whispered. "Just small town living. No one is saying anything mean; they're just curious."

Chloe nodded but it did little to ease her mind. Marge came back by and took drink orders for everyone, including the ones not here yet and was delivering them when they got there.

"Perfect timing as always," the new lady told Marge and kissed her cheek.

This must be Macy, Chloe thought.

Macy scooted her chair in on the other side of Chloe, leaving her flanked between Kristin and Macy now. The only bright side to this was there was now a baby next to her to distract her from the people looking at her.

"She's three months old today," Macy said. "Do you want to hold her?"

"I would love to," Chloe said genuinely and smiled for the first time since arriving.

The baby did distract her. She started to relax just a bit, listening to the conversations at the table. Kristin and Macy talked around her, occasionally asking Chloe a direct question. The men chatted about work and kids.

"So, I got the scoop from Kristin, but I want to know, are you thinking of sticking around?" Macy asked.

"I don't know," she answered.

"It's better than the hard no you were at the other night," Kristin added.

"I agree. He looks so happy tonight," Macy said. "He's usually a friendly person and makes everyone laugh all the time, but there's something there all the time that you know he's missing something. It's gone tonight."

Chloe looked up to find David looking back at her. His eyes were dark and she felt the heat emanating from him across the table. Blushing, she turned her attention back to the baby.

"I saw that," said Kristin.

"Me too," Macy teased.

"I'm thinking we should start a club. We should call ourselves the Real Fake Wives," Kristin told the other women.

Macy snorted and tipped her head back trying not to spit out her drink. Chloe laughed too, both at the club idea and at Macy's predicament.

"Don't mind her. Her company all day is first graders and sometimes she acts like one," Macy told her.

"You're a teacher?" Chloe asked.

"Yep. That's how I met Macy initially. I didn't know she was renting my brother's house at the time though."

"That's neat. What do you do, Macy?" Chloe asked.

"I waitress here when Marge needs the help, but I go to school full-time mostly. Just started this semester."

"That's awesome. I want to go back to school sometime."

"What's stopping you?" Kristin asked.

"Spare time." Chloe sighed. There was never enough hours in the day. "And all this mess that's popped up."

"Yeah this is a distraction right now, but when all this gets settled, I'm sure David would help you so you can go back to school."

Macy shrugged. It was exactly what David had offered, but she still wasn't sure how to take it. Maybe it was too good to be true or maybe she was keeping herself from enjoying things. She have to dive into these thoughts later.

"Let me see the baby!" an short older woman in a dress covered in blue flowers said as she walked up to the table.

"The Pillars," Kristin whispered.

Macy took in the other two women with perfectly styled white short hair like the first one. The one in green was a little heavier than the other two, which gave her more of a cherubic face. The one in yellow looked like she'd been asleep with red eyes and a grumpy look on her face.

"Who are the newcomers?" the green lady asked.

David introduced them again as his wife and daughter. She looked up as he did and noticed the majority of the restaurant looking at them, waiting on their reactions.

"You better not be lying, young man," the one in red said and swatted David with her purse as she walked past him to get back to where she was sitting.

They introduced themselves then. "My name is Ethel," the woman in blue started, "That is Mabel," pointing to the woman in green, "and her sister Matilda," she pointed to the woman in yellow.

Well at least they are color coordinated, she thought.

"Hand over that baby," Mabel said.

Chloe looked to Macy for assurance; she grinned and nodded. "These are their honorary grandmothers."

She gently passed the baby to the older woman who immediately started talking to the little girl.

"Now, you're married to that one, huh?" Ethel asked.

It was the first time that she'd had to confirm it, and it felt weird to say it out loud in front of him so she just nodded.

"Speak up, we don't bite," Ethel said.

"Yes, ma'am."

"Oh, manners on this one. I like her."

"I resent that. I have manners," Kristin said.

"Not outside work. When was the last time you said ma'am to me?" Ethel scolded.

"Humph." Like a petulant child, Kristin crossed her arms and sat further back in her chair.

"Now, when did you get married?" Ethel asked, pulling up a chair and clearly intending to stay a while.

"Just answer, it's easier that way; she'll have the story she wants regardless of your desire to tell it," Macy pretended to whisper.

"Yes, I will," Ethel said proudly.

"We got married five years ago," Kristin answered, knowing the next question.

"Where have you been then?" Ethel asked, squinting her eyes to study Chloe.

"Did you think I was always working?" David jumped in. "I was going to visit them."

Chloe prayed that Sadie didn't dispute his story and took a glance down the table to see that she was fully engrossed in a story with Matilda, showing her doll off proudly.

"Why didn't you bring her here before now?" Ethel was on the scent of a story and she knew she was being lied to—you could tell by the way she asked the question so casually, looking between them both, but her eyes dared them to tell another lie.

"How about if we save that story for when we aren't in a crowded restaurant?" David asked.

With one nod she accepted this. "You will tell me what's going on. The three of you," she pointed at the men, "have already lied to us enough."

"I didn't," David defended.

"You just did," Ethel called him out.

"We really are married, I swear." David held up both palms in defense.

"That I do believe," Ethel conceded. She turned her full attention to Chloe once more. "Tell me, did you get a big wedding?"

"No ma'am. We got married at the courthouse."

"Shame on him," Ethel chided. "How about a bachelorette party and shower and all that?"

The women next to her groaned and Kristin was rewarded with a playful slap on the leg from Ethel.

Chloe shook her head. "We were, umm, in a hurry." To drive her point home, she gestured to Sadie.

Understanding lit the woman's eyes. "Well, those things do happen. Such a shame though, the bachelorette party is the best part. These two had fun at theirs."

"I think you enjoy them way more than we do," Kristin said under her breath.

"Hush you," Ethel told her. "I know!" she exclaimed. "We should have a girls night out, and that can be your wedding party. We can pretend you're the bride-to-be."

Chloe waved her hands in protest and shook her head. None of this was necessary and she really didn't want to anyway.

"You can't argue," Macy told her. "Once they get it in their heads to do something, you're just along for the ride."

"You'll have fun. It will be the best thing this year." Ethel got up and put her chair back, spreading her good news to her friends.

"In the end, it will be fun, just know that under those flowery dresses are three horny teenage girls," Kristin told her.

Chloe, who had been taking a sip of her drink, lost it back to her cup. "What?" she choked out.

"Oh, at mine, they danced with the strippers." Kristin laughed. "It's funny now, but at the time it was embarrassing as all get out."

"They made me giant pink inflatable penises," Macy added.

"Oh no," Chloe said as she debated a way out of this.

As though reading her mind, they both assured her she was stuck and just to try to have fun. Chloe sank down in her seat; her life definitely wasn't boring.

They finally ordered once the Pillars had gone on their way. After getting their food, the men finally jumped in on Ethel's idea.

"I don't want to," she confessed.

"You'll have fun if you go," David told her. "If you really don't want to then you can back out; we will come up with something."

On the one hand, she was definitely not looking forward to whatever the night could bring, but on the other, it had been so long since she'd hung out with friends that a girl's night sounded amazing.

She knew she could trust David with Sadie, something that she hadn't ever had. Maybe going wouldn't be such a bad thing. If it didn't go well, at least she had tried, right?

They finished eating and said their goodbyes before heading out to the parking lot. She buckled Sadie in and David handed her his phone and headphones before walking her to her door.

"Chloe."

"Yeah?"

"You really don't have to go if you don't want to," he assured her, his hands rubbing her arms.

"I think I might want to. It could be a good time."

"They're a force of nature." He shook his head.

Chloe laughed. They certainly were that.

9

The day after their dinner at the diner, David had gone out and gotten Chloe a new cell phone. Hers was broken beyond repair and was out of data.

She'd tried to decline it, but he'd insisted, and she spent an hour setting it up. While she had been doing that, she hadn't noticed the tablet that he'd bought Sadie and had set up for her.

"We might travel or something," was his defense.

"The odds of that are so slim. You have to stop buying things for us," Chloe told him.

"I can afford it," he argued.

"I never mentioned the money. You need to stop. We have things now, David. Please just ease up on the buying things, for both of us?" she begged.

"I want you guys to have everything you need and want," he said and dropped onto the couch next to her.

"I understand that and we do. We don't need everything though. She has toys she hasn't even opened yet. We just needed to be safe, and you have given us that and more."

She let her head drop onto his shoulder next to her. This man wanted to make sure they were taken care of. He'd shown that when he married her, when he'd sent money even though she wasn't using it, when he'd taken them in and claimed them both just days ago.

Without wanting to, and despite her best efforts, she was wanting more. She wanted to wake up to him in the kitchen with coffee ready. She wanted to see him playing with Sadie. She wanted him.

The realization hit her like a ton of bricks and she quickly rose, leaving David on the couch. She went upstairs to his room that she'd taken as her own.

She just needed a few minutes, she told herself, just a few minutes to clear her head and remember that her not staying was to help David and that she needed to not be selfish. David deserved the opportunity to choose his future, not have one forced on him.

"Hey," David was gently knocking on the door.

"One second," she said as she tried to wipe the tears from her cheeks. "It's open."

Keeping her back to him, she busied herself with looking through a drawer of her clothes.

"What did I do?" David asked.

The pleading in his voice had her tears back full force. "You didn't do anything wrong. It's just me."

"Talk to me, Chloe," he pleaded.

"I can't," she sniffed.

"Let me in. I can help."

"I know you can. I just don't want you to have to."

She turned to him then, and he immediately wrapped her in a hug.

"I don't know what you want from me."

"More than I deserve," she said as she relaxed into his arms.

They stood there, him letting her cry it out again as time passed. When she thought she was done, she backed away from him.

"Please tell me what's going on," he asked.

"I don't even know anymore." He looked sad and she wanted to help, but she couldn't help herself at this point. "Let me think for a few days, and I will discuss it with you. I need to figure myself out first."

She could tell he wanted to say more; his mouth opened and then closed. He looked her up and down before taking a step back.

"I wish I could make you understand that I don't want to hurt you," he said.

"I know that. I really do," she told him. "I don't want to hurt you either, and I am scared that I am going to."

David dropped his head and left her standing in his room. There were no more tears for her to cry, nothing but her own thoughts as she struggled to do what she thought was the right thing: keep her distance from David.

She spent the rest of the morning in her room, texting with Kristin and Macy about the plan for the girl's night tonight. She nearly backed out but thought that some space between her and David might help settle her thoughts.

None of them knew where they were going, but apparently the Pillars had rented a limo so no one had to drive. After learning the details of the previous two bachelorette parties they had thrown, Chloe joined the other two women with their suspicions and fears of the night ahead.

She left her room to make lunch for Sadie and ran into David in the kitchen. He offered her a plate of the lunch he was already making, and they all sat at the table.

"I love it here," Sadie said as they sat down.

"I'm glad, Sadie girl," David told her, looking at Chloe as though she was breaking his heart.

"I'm happy you love it here too," Chloe told Sadie genuinely.

"We are going to have pizza and watch movies in the living with popcorn tonight. Daddy said!"

"You are?"

"Yep, and Daddy's friends are coming over so we can all play."

"That sounds really fun. I'll miss you."

"I'll miss you too, Momma."

David didn't say anything but she felt him still watching her. She finished her plate and did the dishes before they spoke again.

"If you need anything, please call me?" David said.

"I will, but I can't imagine this night getting that out of hand."

"Me either, but just promise?" he asked.

"I promise, if anything happens, I will call you."

Satisfied, David turned to leave. "I will take good care of her—you know that, right?"

"I wouldn't be leaving her here if I didn't think that." She stopped wiping down the counter and looked at David. "I haven't left her with anyone outside of daycare ever. This is a big deal for me to give you that trust with her, and I haven't doubted that decision in any way."

"Thank you for that," he said and left.

She got ready a little later and was putting finishing touches on her hair when Kristin and Macy arrived. They brought some makeup since she had told them she didn't have any.

The three of them sat on David's bed and helped her get her makeup together. She was thankful they hadn't brought up her and David at all.

"The limo will be here in 15 minutes," Kristin told them, checking her phone.

"I'm nervous," Chloe admitted.

"You don't even know them. I'm terrified." Macy laughed. "It will be an interesting night if nothing else. Plus we get to go out childless for a bit." She looked at Kristin and laughed, "well, mostly."

Kristin threw her jacket at Macy and all three laughed.

"Momma?" Sadie said as she came in the room.

"What's up baby?" Chloe asked.

"I want to get ready too," she said.

That's all it took and all three women helped Sadie put on the smallest bit of makeup and some bright red lipstick that was sure to give David a heart attack. They chatted and held up a mirror for her, and then she went and picked out her favorite dress to wear to eat pizza and watch movies.

All the men assured Sadie they loved her makeup before getting her settled with the baby in the living room so the women could leave. Chloe said her goodbyes before she settled in and the limo pulled up.

"Remember—" David started.

"I promise I will call if I need anything." Chloe finished for him.

"Thank you."

"No. Thank you for caring," she told him.

"Be safe," he told her and then pulled her into the kitchen.

"What are you doing?" she asked.

"You forgot something."

"What?"

"This."

His mouth found hers again, and she felt the emotion in the kiss all the way to her toes. Her arms came up around David's neck without hesitation as she clung to him, letting herself go to the kiss.

He broke it off as quickly as he started it and rested his forehead on hers. "Go." He told her, his voice rough and deep.

She nodded and ran out the door, jumping into the waiting limo. Everyone was laughing as she did, and even though they didn't see the kiss, they all knew what had kept her.

"Drink up!" someone said pushing a glass of wine into her hand.

"We were going to do champagne but none of us like it, so we did wine," Ethel said proudly.

"Where are we going?" Chloe asked.

"It's a surprise."

They drove for a bit, but with Chloe not really knowing the area at all, she had no idea where they might be headed. Looking out the window, she nudged Macy next to her to look as well.

"Oh my God," was her reaction as the Pillars grinned and grabbed their purses.

"Let's get out then, I guess we are here!"

"You're joking?" Chloe asked to no one in particular.

"It's about to be the best night of your life!" Mabel said and followed Ethel out of the limo.

10

$\mathcal{M}$acy and Kristin had to help Chloe get out of the limo as she looked around, taking in the dark parking lot, contrasted by the bright lights on the building and a huge sign that said *Ladies Night.*

"This... this isn't real," Chloe said.

"I never thought they would—didn't even think of it." Kristin admitted.

"It's a strip club!" Macy said, still a little shocked.

Three short white-haired women were already lining up to go inside and waving at them to hurry. Their smiles were taking up their whole faces, and at this point, Chloe had to go along just because they were so excited.

"We aren't staying long, right?" Macy asked.

"We let them provide the ride," Kirstin said and huffed out a breath.

As they went into the club, the music, which had been dull outside, was suddenly palpable. Every beat was felt.

"Let's get our seats!" Ethel said and pulled Chloe along to a table that was right in front of the stage, dead center.

A pink sash that said *Bride-to-be* was placed over Chloe and a crown was put on her head. Chloe wasn't given a chance to think about it before she was being pulled on stage to loud shouts from the crowd.

Two very scantily dressed men led her to a chair in the middle of the stage and another with a microphone let the crowd know that she was about to get married and was here to celebrate. None of that was true, of course, but she was warned that they were going to pretend.

She looked out to the crowd, searching for her friends, but was blinded from seeing anyone by the bright white stage lights. The man continued to talk, hyping up the crowd before music started playing.

Nervous wasn't a good enough word for how she was feeling. She was completely and utterly terrified of what was going to happen. She'd never been to a strip club in her life and while she had seen a movie or two, she still didn't know what to expect.

More men, with more clothes on, came out from backstage and started dancing to the music on the stage. They each took a turn getting entirely too close to her before going back to dancing.

Looking around, she promptly squeezed her eyes shut as the men ripped their shirts off and threw them behind them. She was sweating now too and gripping the chair for strength, knuckles white. She wanted to flee the stage.

One man, over six feet tall with washboard abs, started dancing close to her. Suddenly, he was in front of her and his pants went flying.

She let out an "oh" that was more of a squeak as she tried to focus on any other part of the man except his package being presented to her over and over to the beat of the music.

He danced his way behind her. She didn't know what he was doing, but the yells from the crowd told her it was something that everyone else was enjoying. He rolled his hips around over and over as he made his way back to the front of her and took one of her hands to place on his chest.

"Give it up for the bride-to-be!" the man with the mic said, and the crowd yelled again.

The man who was dancing in front of her led her back to her seat. It was over, thankfully.

"Girl, you handled it better than I would have," Kristin said.

"Glad it looked like it. I don't even know what just happened," Chloe told her.

"Did you have fun?" Mabel yelled over the music across the table.

"Sure?" she said, but it was more of a question.

"If we are lucky, this will be the end of that for the night," Kristin leaned in to tell both Chloe and Macy.

"I need a drink," Chloe said.

"I think we get servers here, or do we go to the bar? Because me too." Macy looked around for any idea of how to get one. "I'm going to the bar," she finally said.

"I'm coming." Chloe stood to go with her.

"I might not be able to drink, but you aren't leaving me here alone," Kristin yelled catching up with them.

At the bar they yelled a drink order and waited. She was going to have such a headache by the end of the night from the loud music.

"Should we have left them alone?" Chloe asked.

"Probably not, but they're adults and we have a driver." Macy shrugged.

"They're going to end up on stage," Kristin said.

Taking their drinks, they made it back to the table just in time for another show. It was easier to appreciate and play along when you weren't the center of attention, Chloe thought.

She and her friends cheered along with the crowd for the show. Honestly, the ability to get that many men who could dance and looked like that in one spot was kind of impressive on its own.

"We have money!" Matilda yelled, shaking a wad of ones.

Fortunately, no one jumped off stage to take her up on her bills. As Chloe sipped her drink, she relaxed more and so did Macy. Before too long, they were just as loud as the rest of the crowd as Kristin rolled her eyes at the both of them.

"Y'all are going to get me in trouble," she told them.

"How?" Chloe asked.

"Because your husbands are going to be pissed and I am the sober one," she laughed.

"Do you think David will be upset?" Chloe hadn't considered that David might not be happy about the choice of entertainment for the night.

She reached in her purse and fumbled for her phone only to drop it on the floor. She picked it back up and quickly pulled up David's messages.

"I'm teasing, Chloe," Kristin told her. "No one will be mad, and he knew we were going to get into something crazy with those three."

She pointed to the Pillars who were still actively waving money to try to entice the dancers off stage.

"I'm just going to go check on Sadie," she said, and taking her phone, she left the table.

No one followed her and she was grateful for that. Stepping outside where the music was only dull, she called David.

"Everything okay?" he answered.

"It's fine. I just wanted to check on Sadie."

"She's great. I can't believe she ate so much pizza, but she's good."

"Oh, great." She didn't know what else to say and the call went completely silent.

"What's going on, Chloe?"

"It's stupid. Everything is fine, I just..." She just what? Did she even know?

"Just what, baby?" David asked.

"They took us to a strip club," she blurted out.

David laughed. "They are the strangest three women."

"Are you, umm, like, does that bother you?"

She heard David moving on the other end of the phone. "I'll be right back," he told someone else, probably the other guys. "Chloe, why on Earth would I be upset?"

"I don't know, but I needed to be sure."

"Even when I convince you this is really what I want, Chloe, I'm not going to be upset over this. Enjoy yourself, have fun. I will be here, with Sadie, who will hopefully be asleep when you get back."

"Okay."

"Chloe, really, it's not an issue."

"I just wanted to talk to you for a second I think."

"I can stay on the phone with you if you want," he offered.

"I'm good now. I'm sorry."

"Sorry for what?" he asked but didn't give her a chance to answer. "We can unpack all this another time. If you're ready to, you can go back with them, or I can come get you, or I can just stay on the phone. It's entirely up to you."

"I'm going to go back to the table. Thank you for talking to me."

"Always."

She ended the call feeling silly but better about being there. Showing her stamp to the bouncer, she let herself back in and headed for the table when Macy approached her.

"Don't go there without another drink," she said and pulled her to the bar where Kristin was waiting.

"What—" She looked out towards their table to find each Pillar with a male stripper getting a dance to themselves and sliding dollar bills into places she didn't want to think about.

"Are they? Is this for real?" she asked, taking her drink from Kristin.

"Do you know how much I want to drink some of that right now?"

"Can't be any more than I do," Chloe said.

"This is gonna be so good." Macy handed her drink to Kristin and pulled her own phone out.

"What are you doing?" Kristin asked.

"Taking photos."

She snapped a bunch and then started a group chat with the husbands and wives to send the pictures of these three women dressed in their Sunday best sticking dollar bills in men's pants.

Immediately, all their phones went off as the husbands all replied.

Why would you send that?

This is bullshit.

Do not send more.

All came through at one time. Chloe laughed as she read them and some green faces came through.

I had to see it so you do too.

Macy sent the last message and put her phone away. The strippers had left their table so it was time to sit back down.

"You guys missed all the fun," Ethel said.

"Let's call them back over," Mabel suggested.

"No!" Chloe, Kristin, and Macy all yelled at the same time.

"You guys are young enough to enjoy life more than us. You really need to lighten up," Matilda told them.

"Never as young as you," Kristin said, which earned her big smiles from all three Pillars.

The rest of the night passed with more shows, but thankfully, no more lap dances. They didn't stay super late, the Pillars declaring it was past their bedtime at ten o'clock. Chloe laughed; it was past hers too.

All three husbands were on the porch as the limo stopped to drop them off. Each man came out to claim his wife as she climbed out of the limo.

"Macy's drunk!" Kristin yelled when she got out.

"I am not," Macy denied and then fell out of the limo.

"Dear God," Daniel said, trying to help her up.

"I've got this, there was something there," Macy said.

"There's nothing there," Daniel said on a laugh.

Chloe climbed out behind her once she was out of the way. David was there as soon as she stood up.

"I am not drunk," Chloe laughed as she watched Macy try to get in Daniel's truck.

"Hmm," David said, assessing her.

"I had two drinks, didn't finish the second, and a little bit of wine on our way there."

David laughed. "I wasn't accusing you of anything else."

"You were wondering."

"Maybe," he admitted. "Sadie is in bed already."

"I hope she wasn't any trouble for you guys."

"None," he said with pride.

They stood on the porch and waved to everyone as they left. She ended up having a really good time but was also happy to be done for the night.

11

———————

"Did you want to watch a movie or something or are you ready for bed?" David hoped she wanted to hang out a bit, but understood if she'd rather not.

She shrugged and laughed. "Both?"

"That could be arranged." He said jokingly. With a laugh, he locked the door and turned off the lights to head upstairs as well.

"I need to shower, but okay." He heard her say.

His first thought was it was a good thing the lights were out because he felt his eyes pop open and his jaw drop. "What?"

"Let's watch a movie upstairs." Chloe said way more casually than he felt.

"Umm," he swallowed, trying to be calm, "okay."

"You get it set up. I'll shower real quick." She walked up the stairs and went into her room, and David went into his own.

He grabbed the small dresser in the room with both hands and took a steadying breath. He didn't know what this meant, but he felt like a teenage boy again, going out with a girl for the first time.

Once he felt like he had regained some composure, he let go of the dresser and dug out some clothes. Changing quickly into some shorts and a clean shirt, he tucked a condom he'd bought the other day into his pocket and grabbed his pillow.

In her bedroom, he sat on top of the covers, laid back against the pillow and headboard, and started searching for movies to watch on the streaming service. He heard the shower turn off and had to adjust his seat, nerves creeping back up again.

She was out of the shower and in the room in no time flat. "Hey." She greeted him as she walked in, still brushing her hair.

"Hey." He immediately regretted the lame repetition of what she said instead of saying anything else.

She sat the brush down and drew back the covers, sliding in next to him and getting comfortable. "What'd you find to watch?"

"Nothing yet. What are you in the mood for?"

"Doesn't matter."

"Helpful," Daniel teased.

"Just pick something." She told him.

He had no idea when he clicked on. The scent of her shampoo, fruity and sweet, was drifting up to his nose, and it was overwhelming all his senses.

Having clicked on something, he set the remote between them, a weak barrier, letting her know he didn't intend to cross the line with her.

"Aren't you cold?" She asked him.

"A little. I might go get a blanket in a bit."

"Get under the covers, then." She rolled her eyes.

"Chloe," his voice gravelly even to his own ears. "I'm trying really hard here."

"Oh, fine." She tossed the covers back and climbed over him, straddling his legs and sitting on his lap.

"Chloe." He ground out as he gripped the covers, attempting to keep his hands off her.

"David," she answered.

"I think maybe you had more to drink than you thought." David didn't know how to disentangle himself from her without touching her.

"I did not. I just want this." She looked down at him and he knew his face was strained as he held tight onto his last thread of sanity. "Oh, my God. I'm sorry, did I misunderstand?" Her face flamed red as she tried to quickly climb off of him.

He grabbed her hips and returned her to his lap. "Does it feel like you misunderstood?" He asked and ground his erection against her.

"N-No," she answered.

"I've got very little control of myself at the moment, so be sure you mean this." He warned.

"I want this." She assured him and reached up, tossing her shirt to the floor.

He groaned and, using one hand, he cupped the back of her neck, pulling her mouth down to meet his. The kiss was hungry, heated, and intense.

His left hand crept up to her bare breast. She moaned into his mouth as he cupped it, giving it a few squeezes. Her body pushed into his hand as he released her mouth and she tossed her head back.

As she arched further towards him, David broke the kiss, instead trailing gentle kisses down her neck, taking care to go as slow as possible, reveling in the way she reacted to each one. Her body shivered with each small kiss, her hands tightening in his hair as he made his way to her breasts.

Kissing the tops of each breast, he used both hands to squeeze and lift them closer to his face. He used his right hand to find her nipple as he used his mouth to find the other. As he drew it into his mouth, Chloe cried out.

"That's enough of that." He placed his arms around her and turned them both so she was now lying on the bed with him above her.

He backed away as shy let out a small protest and her hands grabbed his arms to pull him back.

Chuckling, he pushed her arms away. "I'm just taking my shirt off, too." Tossing it to the floor with hers, he looked his fill.

He had answers to the question he'd wondered for years. Her skin flushed all over, it didn't stop at her neck. He had the urge to taste that flushed skin, and follow it wherever it may lead.

"David?" She pulled him from his perusal of her body. "I haven't — that is, I don't — "

"Whatever it is, it's okay." He meant it wholeheartedly.

"I don't know if I will be any good at this. I've only been with the one person."

Mentally, he thanked her for not using his name. "Honey, there is no way you could be bad at this. Just follow your instincts and enjoy it."

She bit her lip, causing his hard cock to press at his now too tight shorts. Thankfully, he hadn't stayed in his jeans tonight.

Covering her body with his, he kissed that worried lip free. "You tell me if I do something you don't like, and I'll do the same, okay?" He doubted there was anything she could do he wouldn't like, but wanted her to feel comfortable.

"Okay," she breathed, as David returned his attention to her two white breasts, eager for his touch. "Please don't stop." She begged.

"I've barely started," he promised.

He slid his hand further down, over her shorts, applying pressure where he knew she needed it most. Her hips bucked under him as she searched for her pleasure.

"That's it, baby." He encouraged as he raised his head to watch her face.

"I need more." She closed her eyes tightly as she continued to rock her hips.

"What do you need?" He asked, wanting to hear her say it.

Her eyes flew open, and despite the haze of desire, he could see her focus on him. "You. I need you."

"Let me help you out, then." He teased and backed away to remove his shorts and pull on the condom he had brought.

She wiggled out of her shorts on the bed and studied him as he rolled the condom on. Her gaze was like a caress to his cock as it reached out towards her, begging to give her what they both wanted.

He climbed back onto the bed, spreading her legs open for him as he slid between them. He leaned over to kiss her as his tip touched her entrance.

Slowly, almost painfully slowly, he slid into her. He knew he wouldn't last long, this moment he'd dreamt of for so many years finally here, but she seemed on the edge as well.

Next time, he thought, next time he would take his time. Tonight, now, he needed her too badly. Puling all the way out, he thrust back into her in one push, Chloe crying out as he did.

He waited for her to tell him it hurt, thinking he may have been too rough. When she didn't and instead only tried to move her hips below him, he did it again.

Her heat was surrounding him fully with each thrust. Her body pulsing around him, bringing them both to the brink of pleasure. He slid his hand down between them and found her clit. Using a firm circular motion, he rubbed until he saw her grow more frantic.

"Let go." He urged.

"David—I..." she trailed off as he felt her body tense around him.

He pumped faster, riding her wave of pleasure to his own peak, before ducking his head into the pillow beside her as he felt his own release.

His body jerked, spent, as he attempted to catch his breath. He rested on his forearms above her, try to keep from crushing her.

He searched for something to say and instead just kissed her before sliding out of and away from her. She stretched, not looking up at him as he climbed out of the bed, and dragged the used condom off and dropped it into the trashcan.

Chloe rolled onto her side and he slipped on his shorts before climbing in behind her and draping one arm across her waist. This was a night he'd remember forever, he thought, as he closed his eyes and drifted to sleep.

12

———

*D*avid slipped from the bed early the next morning to go downstairs before Sadie woke up. Sitting in the living room so he could see the stairs, he checked his emails.

The private investigators had come through with a copy of the will. Skimming through it, he didn't notice anything that stood out to him, but it was all legal speak and very long. There was so much money being doled out in the will, properties and businesses not included.

Now he needed the lawyer to translate it. He forwarded that over to the lawyer he'd already hired in case of a custody suit that was surely coming. Chloe didn't know he was already that prepared, but he saw no reason to wait for the inevitable.

Then he checked his work emails and wrote his bosses back that he would be ready to assist on the next job that came up, from here. There was no way he was going back to traveling, especially now with Chloe and Sadie here.

But how long would they be here? He wondered. What was it going to do to him when they did leave? One thing was certain, he needed to do everything he could to convince Chloe not to leave.

Last night, though. Last night had been amazing. It was everything he wanted it to be, dreamt it would be, and more. Once he'd been certain she wasn't drunk, he let her lead the night, and oh what a night it was.

He stretched. It had been a while since he had been with a woman, but being with her had been mind-blowing, and he didn't think time had anything to do with it. It was better than he'd imagined, and he'd imagined it plenty.

He was going to do everything he could, especially after last night, to convince her that they could make this marriage work in every sense. She and Sadie had always meant a lot to him, but they had come to mean even more now that they were a real part of his life and not just something he thought about.

Sadie came down the stairs carrying her doll in her arms and sat next to him. Though *next* wasn't even the right word—she sat so close to him there was no space between them. He smiled and put her onto his lap.

"What do you want for breakfast today?" he asked her.

Sadie shrugged and rested her head on his chest.

"What if..." He waited for her look up at him. "What if we woke up your mom and went out to breakfast?"

"Yeah!" Apparently that shook the sleep off.

She climbed out of his lap and made for the stairs with David in hot pursuit.

Sadie made it to the bedroom before him and unceremoniously jumped into the bed and onto the no-longer-sleeping Chloe. "Wake up! We are going to get breakfast!"

He was genuinely confused by her excitement, but he'd take it no matter the reason. He didn't interrupt the moment. Instead, he leaned against the doorframe, wishing this was every day and praying for it.

"Back up," Chloe told Sadie as she tried to sit up, taking the sheet with her as she tried to stay covered. Looking at him in the door, she shot him a questioning look.

"I tried to beat her to the room," David said in defense.

She pinched the bridge of her nose and took a deep breath. "Go get dressed and make sure you brush your teeth. I have to get ready too."

"Yes!"

David's heart fell to the ground as Sadie jumped off the high bed and landed on the floor. He was already reaching for her before she hit the ground and, completely oblivious to his panic, hit the ground running and was out of the room as he tried to catch his breath.

"She's a daredevil," Chloe said with a smile.

"I should get a lower bed," David thought out loud.

"You'll do no such thing."

"She could get hurt."

"She shouldn't jump off the bed at any height. Or into it where people are sleeping." She looked at him with her brows raised, clearly letting him know that was a scold on him.

"I didn't know she would get so excited about going out to breakfast," David defended.

"We haven't been out for breakfast many times because it's cheaper to eat at home, so whenever we do, it's a full treat. She gets whatever she wants, never finishes it, and then gets to have it for dinner." Chloe shrugged, the sheet still clutched to her chest.

"Sounds like a plan then." He walked over to her and gave her a slow morning kiss. "Good morning."

"Good morning," she said huskily. "Now get out so I can shower and get ready."

David laughed. "Yes ma'am."

Breakfast was indeed a full affair for Sadie. She ordered three different meals at the restaurant. Chloe had tried to talk her into two instead, but David had, as always, encouraged her to get what she wanted.

In the end, one and a half meals worth of food was brought home to eat for later. Apparently, Sadie had her mind set on which was for dinner already. These were adult meals and he was surprised she ate as much of it as she had, without bursting.

On the way home, she fell asleep. David couldn't help but smile at her sleeping form as they got out at home.

As Chloe came around to help get Sadie out, he pressed her to the car and attempted a kiss. Instead of being receptive as expected, she turned her head, his kiss landing on her cheek.

"Not right now," she told him.

He dropped his arm from her shoulder, and she moved away, careful not to look at him. Why, he didn't know. It was a big difference between this morning and now.

"I'll get her," he offered.

"I've got her," Chloe told him and started unbuckling the still sleeping child.

"I'll go get the door then."

She carried Sadie in and then disappeared herself. David sat at the table, looking over his emails, not retaining anything he read as he tried, unsuccessfully, to focus on anything other than Chloe.

After half an hour of silence and reading the same thing over and over, he closed the laptop and went in search of Chloe. Not only did they need to talk about what she was thinking, but he also needed to tell her about the will.

He found her sitting on his bed, looking at something on her phone. The door was open so he knocked on the doorframe. It was a very different mood from the last time he stood here and peered into his own room.

"Can we talk?" he asked when she looked up.

"We should," Chloe nodded and clicked her phone off.

"What's wrong?" He stepped in to the room, stopping short of going to her and sitting on the other side of the bed instead.

"We shouldn't do this, David. We are pretending to make things work, and I'm scared of what's going to happen when it ends," she told him, without looking at him, keeping her gaze on the blanket.

"Why does it have to end?" He knew it came out as a plea; it wasn't how he intended it.

"Because you didn't sign up for this mess that is my life. I shouldn't have even come here and pulled you into my mess, again." She picked at a thread on the blanket.

"I wouldn't be asking you to stay if I didn't want into that mess. I want this, you, Sadie, all of it." He couldn't understand why she wasn't getting it.

"My life is a mess. It always is, no matter what I do. It ends up in some dramatic bullshit that leaves everything in tatters, and then I have to put it together again. That's not what you want, it's not what you deserve."

"You don't deserve to do everything alone. Let me in, Chloe. Let me help." He reached for the hand that was still picking at the thread, but she pulled it away.

"You want to save us, but I don't think you've really considered what it would mean to do this full time. Eventually, we both have to go back to work. It won't be fun outings and happiness all the time. You deserve a woman who will start their family with you. Someone to fall in love with and build a family, not have one just show up at your door." She had stood and started pacing, keeping her voice low, mindful of the sleeping child down the hall.

"What about you? What do you deserve?" he asked. "You're so worried about what you think is right for me, but what's your thought for you?" The frustrating was creeping into his voice, but he couldn't help it. Everything was all about the misguided thoughts of what was best for him.

"I go back to a life and make things work for me and Sadie." She shrugged.

"What about happiness?" he asked.

"Who says that won't make me happy?"

"Will it? You'll be happiest to leave here and go at it alone?"

"It doesn't matter." She avoided answering.

"It does. It also matters what I want. It matters that I would have made this a real marriage from the beginning. I offered then." And he had again, more than once.

"You're confusing this with some hero complex. You just want to save me, but then what?" she asked.

"Chloe." He stood and took both her hands in his. "If you hadn't been with someone when I finally worked up the nerve to tell you how I felt about you, maybe none of this would have happened."

"You don't mean that. You're not being rational." She started to pull away.

"I do mean that. Look at me." He waited for her to look up at him. "I promise you I mean it."

"We aren't thinking straight. For goodness sake, we didn't even use protection last night!" She dropped her arms to her sides in defeat.

Finally, the root cause of what was bothering her, he thought. "Chloe, we are married. If we made a baby last night, then we will love it and take care of it. If you're scared of that then we won't do it again without protection. If you never want to have sex again, then we won't." He urged her to believe him.

"Stop it. Just stop."

"Stop what?"

"Stop being so..." she used both arms to gesture towards him, "nice." Chloe said with her hands and then spun away from him.

"Let me get this straight. You're upset because I'm being nice and not rushing you out of my life?" David ran a hand through this hair in frustration. It didn't make sense.

"No. Yes. I don't know." Chloe dropped onto the bed. "Why would you want me?"

"Why wouldn't I?"

She glared at him. Clearly that wasn't the answer she wanted, but he wasn't going to back down.

"Chloe, I'm going to convince you this is what I want. It is. Just relax and let me share some of the load?"

"I don't know how," she confessed.

"Let's figure it out together."

"I don't know if I can."

"Let me know when you decide, Chloe."

He left her in the room. He wasn't sure where he stood again, and it was his least favorite place to be—in limbo. It was where he always seemed to end up with her.

13

———

The morning came too quickly after a very awkward day yesterday. She and David had barely spoken to each other, and she'd spent most of the day upstairs hiding from the mess she'd made.

It wasn't that she didn't want to be with David. She definitely did, but they'd forced themselves on him, and she wanted him to have his choice at a better, less messy life, one she certainly didn't have to offer.

Today, she decided as she got out of bed, she would work towards solving their problem and not just waiting it out. She checked on Sadie, still sleeping, and took a deep breath before heading downstairs where she knew David would be.

The scent of coffee drifted up the stairs and she sighed. It was nice being here, having coffee in the morning, being able to sleep in some days because David was always up and never seemed to mind having Sadie around.

Her heart ached as she thought of how Sadie would feel when they left. It had her pausing halfway down the stairs to put a hand to her chest at the ache.

She couldn't, wouldn't trap him in this fake marriage. Even if he meant what he said about always having wanted her, they weren't the same people now. They barely knew each other. Yet, she'd slept with him, but she didn't regret it.

The other night had been amazing. She'd been on such a high, wanting this to work, wanting a happy family, wanting him. God, she wanted him.

David was standing in the kitchen pouring his own coffee when she came in. "Coffee's fresh." He said without turning to her. "I have some information I need to discuss with you about your situation when you have a chance."

"Okay." It was a lame excuse for an answer. She had so much she wanted to say, none of it made sense. None of it came out.

She watched as David finished making his cup and took it with him to the table where his laptop sat. To steady herself and give her something to do with her hands, she poured a cup.

"David?" she started. "Can we talk?"

"Sure, let me just pull this up, and I will show you what I found."

It wasn't what she meant, but maybe it was a good place to start, so she nodded and sat next to him at the table.

"Don't be mad." He finally looked at her. "I hired a lawyer to help us," he cleared his throat, "I mean you."

She hated that David seemed sad. "Okay." That was her word of the day apparently.

"I have Larry's father's will, but I scanned it and I'm not one hundred percent certain I am reading it correctly. I wanted someone that would understand the legal terms to go over it. I have a meeting with the lawyer later today to discuss it."

"Can I see it?" she asked. She wouldn't understand more than him, but she wanted to try.

"It's here." Sliding the computer to her, he got up and paced as she read.

There was something in there about a significant amount of money and a child, but it was worded weird. "Does this mean he needs to have a child to claim his inheritance?" She asked out loud.

"I think so." David confirmed and sat down with her again, taking the computer back. "I just want to be certain."

She nodded. If the only thing that stood between Larry and his money was Chloe, she'd never win. He couldn't have children anymore, last she'd heard, something about cancer, but she hadn't really paid attention to the gossip since it didn't matter to her.

"Take a deep breath. We will have more information later. You worry too much," David told her.

"You don't understand." She took her ponytail down and put it back up again, resetting her brain as she did. "If we are reading that right, we will never win against him."

"We will figure something out, and you can get back to your life."

She nodded. "You know I don't mean to hurt you, right? That's not my intention."

"What is your intention?" he probed.

"Self-preservation." It was a whisper, but it was the full truth, which he deserved.

"Chloe, I'm not trying to hurt you." He reached for her but then stopped and dropped his hand on the table instead.

"I'm not trying to hurt you, David. Even if I let myself think this could work between us, I'm so scared of screwing it up. I don't want you to wake up one day and finally realize what a burden we are on you." She wiped the tears from her cheeks that had started somewhere in that last sentence.

"You aren't a burden. I don't know why you think you are. I want this. Let me in, let me help."

David pleaded with her and she felt her own resistance start to wane. Distance was what she needed. She stood and moved to the sink to clean out her cup.

"I don't know what I am, David. I don't know what my life is even going to be in a week, and all you've done is help me and be incredibly wonderful." She spun from the sink to face him, still at the table. "It feels a lot like I'm using you, like I have been using you for years."

She was, or had been at least. Right now, he wanted a partnership, but how could something like that be built from this? Wanting it wouldn't be enough; she'd seen that her whole life.

"Chloe." David stood and went to her, wrapping his arms around her and pulling her close. "You know that's not how I feel. You don't seem to want to admit that you know it, but you do."

She was a terrible person, but she took his comfort, every ounce he was willing to give her. Putting her arms around him, she held him as they stood there, and she tried to sort the conflicting thoughts in her mind.

"Momma?" Sadie's voice interrupted their hug.

Chloe spun in David's arms and faced the sink to wipe her face and take a deep breath. David stepped away and spoke to Sadie.

"Momma needs a minute. Can you help me with something?"

"Were you kissing?"

David coughed and Chloe debated sticking her whole head in the sink.

"Why?" David managed.

"That's what parents do, right?"

"Sometimes."

Chloe turned from the sink and took in Sadie's small form with David knelt next to her.

"Okay," she answered and skipped off to the living room.

When the sounds of the TV drifted into the kitchen, they both finally moved. David stood and looked at her.

"Are you okay?" He looked her up and down before holding her gaze.

"I'm good. Sorry about that." If the floor opened up and swallowed her whole right now, she'd smile all the way down.

"It's okay, just a kid being a kid." David shrugged.

"Okay. Umm...I'll make breakfast then."

"Thanks, the appointment is in about three hours. I'll let you know when she calls." David went back to his computer at the table.

She busied herself with breakfast, then with Sadie, and got ready for the day. Nothing had settled between her and David, but she couldn't help but feel like somehow, some things had changed in a good way.

A few minutes before twelve o'clock, she made sure Sadie was content with her tablet and toys in her room. "I love you. Stay up here while we have a phone call, okay?"

Sadie nodded, not even looking up.

Chloe closed the door and went to find David. He had the computer open again on the table with two notepads.

"Have a seat. I got you something to take notes with. I'm going to as well; we can compare after."

"Okay." She bit her bottom lip and sat down, picking up the pen and clicking it a few times.

"It's going to be okay." David took the pen and sat it on the table.

"You don't know that. I just don't know what I'll do if she is really what he needs to get his money. He'll—"

"Stop, we are going to find out, and then we will worry about what next."

Just then the computer rang, causing her to jump. "Sorry."

David laughed and answered the video call.

After some polite introductions, David thanked the lawyer for meeting them this way and they got down to business. Chloe mostly just listened. She did write a few things down as they went.

"As for the part about the heir, which I assume is the most important part here?" the lawyer asked.

"That's correct," David answered.

Chloe picked up her pen, ready to take any notes that might help them.

"It does state that the son would be required to have a child, but not required to be married, to receive their inheritance."

Her stomach sank. She wrote the information down, but what difference did it even make anymore? She chewed her lip as she felt David's hand come up and start rubbing her back.

"It's a very unusual clause to be certain, but it is legal," the lawyer stated.

"Is there any way around it?" David asked.

"Not specifically, no. Can you tell me more about the situation here? If it applies, I may be able to help."

David gave her a brief rundown of what was going on and how their child fit into the picture. Chloe didn't have anything to add specifically, so she nodded to confirm here and there.

"In that case, I might be able to help." The lawyer smiled.

14

———————

*D*avid was worried. That was an understatement. He was internally freaking out as they waited for Larry and his mother to call.

Oh, he was doing his absolute best to pretend otherwise for Chloe's sake, but she probably recognized the pacing he'd been doing for what it was—when she saw him, that is. She'd retreated to the bedroom not long after they talked to the lawyer and had only come down a few times since then.

The lawyer was going to call Larry and his mom and then put them in touch with Chloe and David. That was the plan anyway if they accepted. It was also possible they would hear from their lawyer instead.

It was a solid plan, one that took a few steps but would allow them to keep Sadie away from Larry and his family for good. It did nothing as far as Chloe's mother was concerned, but other than being nosy and helpful to her friend, she really had nothing to do with it.

The plan also meant that he could stay Sadie's dad in all the ways that mattered, something that he didn't know was as important to him as it was until they showed up. She was now his daughter, and he would move mountains to make sure it stayed that way.

"Any news?' Chloe asked as she came down the stairs.

"Nothing yet. It's only been a few hours though."

"She's taking a nap, so I thought we might talk?" She stepped into the living room but didn't take a seat.

He nodded and held out his palm towards the recliner for her to take a seat. She shook her head.

"I don't know if this will work, but if it does, I can't thank you enough for your help." She was the one pacing now, looking anywhere but at him. "I think if they take this offer, Sadie and I should head back home and try to get our lives back together."

What? he screamed in his head. "You don't have to—"

"It's coming, so it's probably best to go ahead and do it sooner rather than later."

David stood. "Chloe, you... we..." He didn't even know where to start.

"I know we talked about you staying as Chloe's father, and I don't think that would be a problem. I wouldn't ask for child support or anything."

"So, that's it? You're not going to give us a shot?" He walked to the front door, prepared to walk away from the conversation entirely before he said something he regretted. "After all this, you just want to leave? I thought, especially after the other night, that we had something. I guess I was wrong."

He didn't care right now about his phone, the lawyer, anything. He walked out the front door and used all the restraint he had in him not to slam it shut as he did.

There was no plan in leaving, no goal, he didn't even have his keys, so he walked. He walked the neighborhood, lost in his thoughts, ignoring everything else.

She just wanted to leave. He knew she did, but he thought he had more time. He wanted more time to convince her to stay.

Now he wanted to rail at the universe for teasing him with a family and then taking it all away. Right now he had everything he wanted, the wife, the kid, the happy home, only it wasn't happy. Apparently, she was very unhappy—unhappy enough to leave. How was that supposed to make him feel? Maybe it was time to stop wanting her to stay and let her go instead.

He had no idea how long he walked when he finally decided to turn down his street. Opening the front door, Sadie jumped into his arms.

"Where did you go?" she asked.

"I just went for a walk," he told her, kissing the top of her head as he set her back down.

"Next time wait for me," she huffed and folded her arms across her chest, disappointed to have been left behind.

"You got it." He ruffled her hair and she went back to the TV.

Chloe was at the table, writing something in the notepad from earlier. She had to have heard him come in. It would have been impossible not to.

"Did they call?" he asked, seeing his phone on the table.

"Their lawyer did. I advised them to call the one you hired and am waiting to hear back."

That had been the plan. They weren't to speak to the other lawyer to avoid jeopardizing anything.

"Okay."

"David, I didn't try to lead you on. I'm sorry. I am grateful for everything you've done for me, but I'm sorry."

"I want to see her." He'd decided that while walking. "I want visitation."

She set her pen down very carefully and looked up at him.

"I'm not going to fight you for custody or anything like that. I'll keep paying like I have been, and you can use the money or not, but I want to see her."

He had no idea how she was going to react, but if she was going to leave, he needed to know he could still see Sadie. She continued to look at him and didn't speak. He'd give anything to know what she was thinking right now.

"It will give you a break, to work or go to school, or whatever, sleep in?" he urged, listing anything he could think of that didn't mean this was a negative for her.

"David, I..." She picked the pen back up, clicking it a few times before looking at her hand as though she didn't know she was doing it, and set it back down. "I don't want to take your money. I never did. I need you to know that."

"I think the fact that you very rarely used it tells me that. It's yours though, yours and hers. I don't want or need it back. So is everything I bought you two while you were here. I mean it." He took a breath before continuing. "I wanted to do all those things. I want to still do those things, for both of you."

"David, I can't stay." She never would look at him when she talked about leaving.

"I'm trying to respect that, even if I wish that wasn't what you wanted. I am just asking to stay in her life. She means a lot to me, you both do. Please don't take her away from me. We can divorce and share custody, nothing crazy, like every other weekend. I can come to school events and such. That's it."

He was rambling, he knew it. He would get on his knees and beg if that's what it took—anything to keep Sadie from being taken from him completely. The little imp was his daughter, blood or not, and he loved her, wanted and to stay in her life.

"I am sure she will want that," she finally said.

All the air in his lungs came out in a whoosh at the relief of her answer. He thought it would take more convincing than that.

"Thank you. We can set up arrangements with the lawyer after this is settled," he told her and left the kitchen.

He walked down the hall and leaned on wall just outside the living room, watching Sadie play with her doll while keeping one eye on the TV. She was such an animated child, he thought, as she told her doll a story about what was happening on the show.

Looking up, she saw him and smiled. "Come play." She held up a second doll for him.

He smiled back and did exactly as she asked. He sat next to her and played along with her made-up game. It was these moments that he was going to miss not having her here every day.

Chloe stuck her head in the living room. "The phone is for you."

He handed his doll to Sadie. "I'll be back in a little bit." He stood and looked back at her, giving her a smile. "You stay in here for me?"

"Yep," she answered, turning back to her dolls.

"What's up?" he asked Chloe when they were out of earshot of Sadie.

"The lawyer is on the phone." She sat at the table and unmuted the phone and put it on speaker. "He's here with me now."

"Great. David, do you have any questions for me before I start?"

"No, ma'am." He sat next to Chloe and waited.

"Okay. I spoke with their attorney, and we agree this would work and satisfy the needs of the will with the least disruption to Sadie."

He reached over and squeezed Chloe's hand. This was great news, and while he shouldn't have touched her, he was just so excited.

"What will need to happen from here is a DNA test to confirm paternity. I can set that up for you. Once that comes back, we will notify their attorney and send over the paperwork for relinquishing parental rights. After that is signed and I file the paperwork with the courts, we can set up the official adoption for David."

He smiled then. It was the kind of smile that hurt your cheeks, but you couldn't make it stop. He was so excited. It was the best possible outcome.

"And they are good with signing over rights?" Chloe asked.

"Their attorney stated he was. They would also like you to sign something that you will never seek support or anything from them. I'll be honest, it's not necessary once he signs over his rights; you wouldn't have a good case for support, but if you signing it makes them feel better, I would advise to sign it."

"I can sign it today," Chloe offered.

Laughter came through the phone. "I appreciate that, but as your attorney, I would advise you wait until he signs over his rights."

Chloe turned red and David gave her hand another squeeze. "Okay."

"I'm going to schedule the DNA test and then I will email over the details. Let me know if you have any other questions."

"Will it be a blood test?" David asked, worried about Sadie. He'd never been to the doctor with her, but most kids hated shots.

"It's just a mouth swab," she said.

"Thank you. We will wait for your email, I appreciate this so much." David let go of Chloe's hand and picked up the phone.

"Happy to help. Have a good day."

The call ended and David stood. "This is great news."

"It is." Chloe tapped the pen on the notepad.

"What's wrong?" Chloe looked more tense than before the call.

"What if they change their mind once they know the truth?" She chewed that bottom lip again, as she always did when she was stressed.

He knelt next to her and used his thumb to free her lip. "It's going to be okay. We know they are in it for the money, and trying to take her would mean they have to use or even give you some of that money. They won't do that."

Chloe gave a sad smile. "You're right."

15

Three days later, they loaded into David's SUV and began the hour-long drive to get Sadie's DNA test done. She and David had found a rhythm recently that had created more peace between them after meeting with the lawyer.

Both had helped prep Sadie for this appointment, which was probably overkill, but they were worried. It would take time to come back, about a week, which meant they'd potentially be leaving in a week.

She looked out the window and watched the other cars go buy on the highway. The closer it came to leaving, the more she questioned what to do. Thinking that she was using him was driving her need to leave, but the more she replayed everything that had happened since they came to him, she wondered how much of that was true.

It had never been her intent to use him. Ever. It looked like she was though, and she couldn't help but think that was true. At the beginning he had offered the marriage, she had only gone to him to tell him her troubles as a friend, not looking for him to fix it.

Chloe turned to check on Sadie, who was lost in her tablet with headphones on.

"Can I ask you a question?" She faced David.

"Of course." He kept his eyes on the road.

"Why did you marry me?" Even she knew now wasn't the best time for the question, but it was on her mind, and she'd spent too long in her own thoughts recently.

His knuckles turned white with his increased grip on the steering wheel. "I wanted to."

"Wanted to what?" she pressed, expecting him to talk about helping her.

"I wanted to marry you," he answered.

Chloe turned and looked out her window again. It wasn't the answer she expected and now she didn't know what to do with the one she got.

David said nothing else. They parked at the office. The entire process took about fifteen minutes from paperwork to swab, and they were done.

"I think we should celebrate." David smiled as he carried Sadie.

"I did good," Sadie cheered.

"You did very good," Chloe assured her.

"There's a pizza place over there. How about an early dinner?" David offered.

They crossed the street and entered the restaurant. After ordering, David gave Sadie a few quarters and showed her how to play the few video games that the restaurant had. It was early still, so the place was empty.

David returned to the table with Chloe. "Why did you ask me that?"

"What?" Confused, she stared at him.

"You asked me why I married you. Why?" He stared at her, waiting for his answer.

"I needed to know." She turned away from him to watch Sadie. "I needed to know why you offered that."

"Chloe, please look at me for a second."

She turned to face him, making sure she could still see Sadie but focus on David.

"I told you before. I wanted to marry you. I've always wanted you as more than a friend. It was selfish of me to offer that when you were desperate, but I don't regret marrying you."

Blinking back the tears that were threatening, she tried to form words. "I—I—"

She was saved from needing to respond by the pizza being delivered. Sadie returned to the table, and they ate.

It was clear that while she was safe for now; she would not be for long and would need to answer him. First, she'd need to decide herself what she was going to do with that information.

To her surprise, he didn't bring it up again, not when Sadie played some more games before they left, or when they were on the way home. She'd waited for him to say something the whole time, tense, unable to relax, on edge.

Sorting her own thoughts was impossible. She wanted to believe him, but couldn't quite bring herself to do it. It may have been that so little had worked out in her life she couldn't quite believe anything would. It could also have been that she didn't believe him, and her gut was torn.

"You get the door and I'll get her." David said, passing her the keys as he got out.

"Okay," she mumbled.

She opened the front door and held it wide for David to carry a sleeping Sadie inside. The car would put her to sleep anytime she had a full belly.

When Sadie was a baby, she would sometime load her up and just go for a drive to help put her to sleep. There were moments back then where she'd considered just sleeping in the car from exhaustion.

Today, though, although those memories of tiny Sadie brought a smile, it also brought questions. What would it have been like to have someone there for her, to help on those stressful nights when she wanted to cry right along with her baby?

She shut the door and locked it, settling into the living room and scrolling on her phone. David joined her but didn't speak. It wasn't the comfortable silence that they'd had before. It was awkward. She was so aware of him sitting there.

After what felt like forever, but was likely just a few minutes, she couldn't take it anymore.

"Why?" she asked, knowing he would know it was the continuation of their earlier conversation.

He turned on the couch to face her, putting one bent leg up on the couch to turn his full body. "I love you. Always have." He said simply.

She gasped. "What?" she stood.

"I never fit into your world when we were young. I knew that and was happy to have you as a friend instead." He took a breath. "Don't get me wrong, I always hated Larry and jealousy was only a small part of it."

She knew she'd heard him, but her ears had to be lying. There's no way that this man just casually told her he loved her.

"You don't even really know me anymore." She told him.

"I do. I mean, sure, we've both grown up, but I know who you are as a person, and that's what matters."

"I—I..."

"You don't need to say it back, Chloe."

"What if I am just using you? You can't be that sure in this now."

"You aren't."

"You — "

He cut her off. "If you were a bad person, you wouldn't be arguing with me about this. You wouldn't be so concerned about using me." He challenged.

"I don't know what to say." She sat back down, but didn't face him.

"You don't have to say anything. I love you and Sadie, and I want you both to stay."

"I don't know if I can." It was a confession. The reality is that she just didn't know what to do here.

"I know that, too." He dragged a hand down his face, a frustration move she'd seen him do before. "I want you to stay, but I know that you probably won't. It's going to piss you off, but I prepaid a few months' rent for you so you wouldn't lose your apartment while you were here, and could go back if that's what you decide."

Like a cartoon, her jaw dropped. He'd made sure she had an out somewhere to go if she didn't want to stay. She hated that he used his money on her again, but at the same time, she appreciated it more than anyone would ever understand.

Never in her life had someone ever just accepted a decision she made. She'd always had to fight her way out of something someone wanted her to do, and she had never had options. David gave her options. He was here if she wanted him to be, but would accept if she didn't stay? What did that mean?

David stood. "I'd like you to stay until we settle everything, but I understand if you can't."

With that simple comment, he walked away, leaving her on the couch with her jaw still open, trying to recover.

By the time she recovered, she was spent. Emotionally, she was drained, and she still didn't know what the right thing was to do. David said he loved her, and she believed he thought he did.

She didn't love him, though. Did she? The pit in her stomach got heavier the more she thought about it. *How would she know if she loved him?* She wondered. She'd thought she loved Larry, but it was clear now that she didn't. What if that clarity comes later with David, too?

Pulling out her phone, she called one of the only two people that she thought might have an answer for her.

"Hey Macy, do you have a minute?" she said as they answered.

"Hey! Of course, what's up?"

16

———————

Two weeks ago, he'd told Chloe that he loved her. It had also been the exact moment that he knew she was going to leave him as soon as they settled the legalities.

They hadn't discussed divorce at all. He couldn't bring himself to bring it up, and figured Chloe would when she got moved out. He didn't want it, but he would not force her to stay. They'd managed a comfortable rhythm in the last few weeks, though.

She got to sleep in, and he got up before Sadie every morning. He was up anyway, so that didn't bother him. Chloe cooked all the meals except breakfast and while the tension wasn't there constantly, it was in the background more often than not.

He'd gotten a fresh case yesterday from work, and that had been a great distraction from the separation that he knew was coming.

"Good morning." Chloe poured her cup of coffee this morning.

"Good morning." He waited for her to sit before talking. "I will probably spend the day in my office today on work, so I won't be able to hang out with Sadie."

"Oh, okay." He watched her smile slip before pasting it back on again. "I will try to keep her quiet."

"That's not necessary. I just need to do a lot of research."

She nodded and stared into her cup. It was something she did every time they spoke in the morning, like the answer to all of life was in there.

Chloe jumped as David's phone rang. "It's the lawyer."

He answered and put it on speaker. "Good morning. Do I have both of you there?"

"You do." He answered.

"Great. I wanted to let you know the DNA results are in. I went ahead and sent them over with the other paperwork, and I am hopeful to have a resolution this afternoon."

"Great." David told her, but couldn't force the enthusiasm he wanted to convey into his voice.

"I also already drew up the petition for David to legally adopt Sadie and once we have the parental rights waived, I will file those, hopefully as soon as tomorrow."

"Thank you so much for all your help." Chloe spoke.

"You're welcome. Once it's all complete, I will let you know what's next."

The call ended, and they both sat there staring at the now black phone screen.

David broke the silence. "You're leaving?" He asked, knowing the answer.

"I need to do this for me."

He gave her a curt nod before rising and placing his cup in the sink. "I'll be upstairs." He was more curt than he knew she deserved, but he couldn't hold it back anymore.

"Please don't be angry with me." She called as he walked away.

He didn't trust his voice or reactions enough to respond, so he continued walking. He understood she was proving something to herself, but that didn't make it hurt less.

When he'd told her he'd always loved her, he meant every word. He also loved Sadie, without a doubt in the world he would do anything for either of them, but today he needed space.

He sat at his desk in what was currently his bedroom and turned on his computer. The three monitors came to life one by one and he welcomed the work that was awaiting him.

Relentlessly, he'd worked the day away. Once Sadie had slipped in and then declared his work boring before leaving him alone again. His team had been worked just as hard today.

Instead of just researching, he'd put the team to doing their own work on the case. They needed to protect a young socialite from potential kidnappers and herself. It wasn't a tough case, and one he'd usually find boring.

"What is wrong with you?" Mike said as David answered the phone.

"Nothing." He said gruffly.

"Don't lie to me. You are always the one smiling, pulling us all out of whatever bad mood we are in, and now you're scaring people."

"Some people need thicker skin."

"Maybe, but what the hell is the problem?"

David leaned back in his chair and stretched. For the first time, he noticed it was now dark outside. "She's leaving." David told him.

"What? Why?" Mike's shocked voice asked the same questions he asked himself constantly.

"She thinks if she stays, she won't be giving me a choice, forcing a family on me."

"Damn dude." There was a long pause before Mike said anything else. "Tell her how you feel, man."

"I did. Two weeks ago."

"Shit."

"Yeah. Look, I've got this case to work on, so I'll talk to you another time." He didn't commit to calling him back.

"Let me know if I can help with anything."

"Will do." David ended the call before Mike could say anything else.

The spell he'd been in while focused on his work was now broken. It had been a long time since he'd spent the entire day at the computer without a break.

Hoping that Chloe wasn't downstairs, he made his way to the

kitchen to get something to eat. His hopes were dashed, though, when he saw her sitting at the table on her phone.

"Let me call you back." She quickly told whoever she was talking to and set the phone down.

"You didn't have to do that. I'll just be a minute." Opening the fridge, he searched for something to eat.

"Can we talk?" Chloe asked.

"Are you still leaving?" he countered, shutting the fridge and crossing his arms.

She nodded.

"Then there's nothing to talk about right now. Once I adopt Sadie, we can talk about whatever this marriage is and how to proceed. I want to see her. I wasn't kidding."

"I didn't think you were." Her voice was small, quiet, and he knew he was going too far.

"Look, I need to process this. I'm not trying to be a jerk, but I can't go on and keep trying to pretend like I didn't have everything I wanted, and it's all about to go away. I need to process this my own way, same as you."

"I understand," Chloe nodded. "I never, ever, dreamed I'd hurt you. I don't want to."

"That much I do know. But if this decision hurts all three of us, is it the right one?" He grabbed a granola bar and left her sitting at the table on the verge of tears.

Had he stayed for another second, she would be in his arms, him trying to wipe her tears away as she pretended she wasn't crying. He poked his head in Sadie's room and smiled at her, sleeping in her too big bed, curled up with three of the dolls he'd gotten her.

Quietly, he closed her door back and went to his office again. He wanted to slam that door. Wanted to yell and curse and fight. He wasn't a fighter, ever. He could fight, if he had to, but he preferred to smile and deescalate.

After an hour had passed, he heard Chloe come up the stairs. She stood just outside his door and he held his breath. He didn't even know what he wanted her to do at this point. Part of him begged her to knock, the other wanted her to go away and stop breaking his heart.

Finally, she knocked. "Come in."

"I just wanted to let you know there is dinner in the microwave for you. Sorry I ran you out of the kitchen earlier."

"Thanks." He said.

"I swear I don't mean to hurt you."

"Chloe, I know that."

"I think it's best if we start getting ready to leave soon, so we don't drag this out."

"Whatever you want to do. Let me know if you need anything."

"Okay," she whispered and backed out and closed the door.

He waited until he heard her close her own door, the door to his own bedroom that he'd probably not sleep in again, before getting up and going downstairs. He looked at the plate, neatly arranged and placed in the microwave for him, and slammed the microwave closed.

Finding his sneakers, he slipped them on and headed for the garage. He needed to do something with his hands, and the garage was the place to do that.

He'd forgotten his garage was occupied with her car. The piece of junk that had barely made it here. Pulling the cover off, since it was no longer necessary to hide her presence here, hadn't been for a while, he stared at it.

If he worked on it, he was only enabling her method to leave him. He wasn't about to let his wife and child leave again in this hunk of junk tough, so he rolled up his sleeves and got to work.

He banged rusted parts off and made notes of ones to get. In the end, it was well past midnight before he had worked off enough frustration to fall asleep. Giving into the exhaustion, he finally carried himself to bed.

17

───────

Chloe set the last box down in her old apartment and sank into her old couch. It wasn't comfortable, she admitted, second hand at best when she'd gotten it, it was a terrible couch. A piece of furniture for the sake of having it.

"That's all of it?" Mike asked.

Mike and Kristen helped her move, as David had been called away with work. He'd likely volunteered because he didn't want to be there when she left. They all knew it.

"That's it." She nodded.

"All right, well, I'll leave you two to it then."

Kristen smiled at her husband and then sat down next to Chloe. "I know we didn't hang out that much, but I'm sorry you're leaving."

Chloe only nodded. What was there to say?

"If you need anything at all, please reach out?" She looked at Chloe. "Promise me?"

"I promise."

"Also, call me when you don't need things?" Kristen teased.

"I will." Kristen told her, not sure if it was true.

"Momma?" Sadie interrupted them. "I don't wanna be back here." She crawled into Chloe's lap and curled up.

"I'll leave you to it unless you want me to stay?" Kristen scooted forward on the couch, her belly now making it hard to get up.

"You guys have done enough already. I really appreciate it."

"Anything for a friend." Kristen told her as she finally stood up. She smiled at Chloe before leaving through the front door.

"When's Daddy coming?" Sadie asked.

It seemed the heartbreak of the day wasn't over yet. "Remember, Daddy doesn't live here? We are going to go back to like it was before and you can talk to Daddy on your tablet and when you get to stay at his house."

"It's not fair! I don't want to not have a daddy anymore." Sadie sprung up off her lap and slammed her bedroom door.

She'd packed up a lot of the toys that David had gotten her, and a few of her favorite outfits, but left things there for her to have when she went to visit. She thought that would make it easier, but it seems there was nothing to ease this transition for her daughter.

Tears came to her own eyes, and she quickly wiped them away. This was the right decision. It had to be. She needed to do this on her own.

A knock on the door had her jumping up from the couch to answer it. She swung the door open without looking and instantly regretted it.

"Mother. How can I help you?"

"I heard you were back and just wanted to come see it for myself. Guess your little marriage experiment didn't work?"

"Not sure what you mean?" Chloe went for ignorance, a practiced emotion she had when it came to her mother.

"Don't play dumb with me, girl. Aren't you going to invite me in? We have quite a bit to catch up on." She moved closer to Chloe, her sickening floral perfume overwhelming Chloe's nose immediately.

"No, I'm not. We just got back, and I have no desire to have a conversation with you now or ever." That felt good. If nothing else, that made her stand a little straighter, proud of herself.

"You can't do that." Her mother put her hands on her hips and tapped the toe of her high heel shoe on the floor.

"I did." Chloe said and slammed the door, locking it behind her.

It took effort, but she managed not to look out the peephole and watch how she reacted. Going no contact with her mother would be hard, but she was going to stand up for herself and keep it that way.

A male voice drifted down the hallway to her. David? She crept down to Sadie's room, peering in the doorway. On video call was David and Sadie, chatting away.

Sadie complained about having to move, and David was doing his best to calm her down. He soothed her worries, reminding her she'd come visit soon, and that she needed to go back to daycare to see her friends.

Another thing David had done for her. He'd paid for daycare for another month. She leaned against the wall and struggled to keep the tears at bay.

"Listen, I need you to be good for you, momma, okay?" David told her.

"Okay." Sadie's watery voice replied.

"I love you."

"I love you too."

Chloe backed away, leaving the door open, and went to the bathroom. She sank against the door and quietly let the tears fall. If this was the right decision, she couldn't help but wonder why she felt so bad about it.

Kristen had asked her today how she would feel if David started dating someone else, and she'd nearly choked. She didn't want to think about that. She had no claim on him, and wanted him to be happy, but the idea of him showing up one day to get Sadie with another woman definitely gave her pause.

She let that emotion wash over her with the frustration and the sadness of the day before she stood. Washing her face, she attempted to make it look like she had herself together.

"Hey kid, wanna order pizza and watch a movie?" She asked Sadie as she left the bathroom.

"Okay," was the reply, not her typical cheerful kid for sure.

Two days ago, she had woken up to an envelope on the table

addressed to her next to her keys. She opened it and considered leaving it there, but had caved and put it in her things.

The cash in that envelope would help with groceries and gas until she got a job, either her old one back or a new one. The other thing in there had been a note, one she hadn't read yet.

She pulled some of the cash out now and called in a pizza order. Sadie was curled up on the couch with a blanket and her three dolls that she refused to leave behind.

"Want to help me put all your new toys away?" Chloe forced a chipped voice.

"No! I want to go home."

And just like that, she'd messed up again and ruined the peace. She handed Sadie the remote instead and ignored the boxes.

She wanted to comfort her daughter, but was scared she'd messed up. This wasn't a feeling she'd had as a parent since Sadie was a baby and she was so scared she'd do something wrong as a new mom.

Now, her daughter was mourning the loss of a father she'd only known for almost two months. Chloe had been the one to take that from her, and she didn't know how to make up for it.

She didn't watch the movie. She let her thoughts wander and let Sadie eat in the living room while watching TV, a rare thing. Once she'd fallen asleep, she picked her up and carried her to her bed, tucking her in and kissing her forehead.

The envelope with the money and the letter suck up out of her purse as she put dinner away. Giving in, she sat at the table and pulled out the letter, unfolding it.

Chloe,

I'm so sorry I couldn't stay. Please know that while I am frustrated, I am not mad at you and I understand that you have something to prove to yourself. I didn't trust myself to let you walk away, so I thought it best that I leave.

Please tell Sadie she can call me whenever she wants and I will answer anytime, day or night, if I'm not at work. Let her take whatever she wants, all of it if she wants to. Tell her I love her.

I know you're going to be mad that there's money in here, but please take it. I know you need it right now having been out of work. It's not a loan, please don't consider that, I know you want to. It's for my wife and child to have whatever they need. I don't want it back.

Send me pictures, I won't bother you with our relationship, please keep me in the loop about what's going on with Sadie. I promise that I do want to be there for her, and you, if you'll let me.

I love you both,

David

She cried like she never had before. Not over her mother, not over Larry, nothing had hurt like this. She had a feeling nothing ever would.

This was heartbreak. She loved him and she'd messed it all up by being too stubborn, and now she didn't know if she could fix it.

18

___

*D*avid sat in his car and stared at his house. It was the last place he wanted to be in the world. He missed them more just looking at it, and he knew it would be worse once he went inside.

He tried to go to Daniel's, but he was in pain and not good company, or so he'd said. Mike was doing something at the school with Kristen, so he'd been forced to come home instead. Now, he'd been sitting here for half an hour, trying to convince himself to go in.

Taking a deep breath, he cut off the engine and stepped out into the cold. He left his bag in the back, just in case he decided not to stay, and headed for the porch.

He fumbled his keys twice before finally getting the right one on the knob and going inside. It was completely dark, something that he'd been used to before and now made him want to cry. He hadn't done that since his uncle passed away.

Being in this empty house felt a lot like he was coming back after a funeral. He sighed and flipped on a light switch, looking around to see what was left.

He grabbed the wall for support as he looked in the living room, nearly falling over. Chloe slept under a blanket on his couch. He said a prayer that this meant what he thought it did before approaching her.

Gently, he shook her arm and said her name. She groaned and reached for the blanket. He couldn't help the little chuckle that slipped out.

"Chloe, baby, wake up," he urged.

At once her eyes popped open, and she jumped up to sitting. "I fell asleep!" She blinked a few times and tried to wake up before rubbing her eyes. "I messed that up, too."

"What did you mess up?" He asked, curious about her intentions.

She made eye contact with him like she was just now realizing he was there. "Crap." She stood up and stretched. "This wasn't how it was supposed to go."

"How what was supposed to go?" He asked again.

"Oh, man. I was trying to surprise you."

"I can confirm that you did."

"I had it planned out." She pouted.

"Want me to go out and come back in? I gotta admit, I'm really curious about what's going on." He looked around at the empty room. "Where's Sadie?"

Chloe blew out a breath. "She's at Macy's."

David felt his hopes rise a little higher. This had to be good news if she left Sadie with a babysitter, right?

"David, back up so I can say what I need to say."

He did as she asked. She stood and faced him.

"I realized after I left that I was making the wrong decision, for Sadie, and for myself. The problem is, I don't think I knew what love was until I was sure I had walked away from it and probably screwed it all up."

He wanted to go to her, to take her into his arms and just hold her, possibly forever. Instead, he waited for her to say what she needed to first.

"I know I never had love from my parents. I was always just an object, almost a pet. I thought I loved Larry, but I realized I never did a long time ago. So when I was here with you, I didn't know what love meant." She took a step towards him. "I came back to apologize to you—"

David stepped towards her. "There's nothing to apologize for."

She held up a palm to him. "Just let me finish, please?"

David nodded and froze where he was, waiting.

"I came to apologize for you, for leading you on when I didn't realize it, and for leaving when I didn't want to because I thought it was the right thing to do. I really thought I was being selfless in leaving, that I was letting you off the hook that you didn't know you were on. But, I got back to the apartment and realized if it was the right decision it wouldn't hurt this bad. And if I hurt this bad, then I can't imagine how much you hurt."

"Chloe," David begged her name. He wanted to go to her, to stop the words and the tears going down her cheeks.

"I love you, David. I'm sorry I screwed up, but I beg you for one more chance, one I won't take for granted. I'll do everything I can to make up all of this to you every single day."

In two strides, he had her in his arms. He didn't care what else she had to say anymore. He needed her now.

"I love you, too." As he brought her into his arms and spun her around the room.

She laughed as he set her back down. "I'm so sorry."

"I love you."

He crushed his mouth to hers, hungry and eager. She returned this kiss with as much passion and love as he'd given her.

Breaking the kiss, they stood there, breathing hard.

"Back up." Chloe placed a hand on his chest and pushed him back a step. "You're messing up my apology and grand gesture."

"I don't need all that, Chloe, just you."

"I want to." She looked up at him and smiled before dropping to one knee. "I'm trying to ask if you would marry me?"

David smiled as he looked down at her and then joined her on the ground. "I think that's my line, but since you asked, yes. Always yes."

ALSO BY TONI DENISE

Learn More at tonidenisebooks.com

Westbeach Series:

Old Friends

On the Run

One Last Chance

Out of Time

Finding Love Series

Engaged to Her Neighbor

Married to the Playboy

Falling for Her Fake Husband

Turn the page for previews

ENGAGED TO HER NEIGHBOR

He didn't want neighbors and she just wanted a fresh start.

Macy is starting over in a new town with her little brother to take care of. She settled on a small town where no one knows their past and they can be themselves without the shadow their father casts over them.

Daniel agreed to rent his property, but it was supposed to be simple instead, a kid and a dog interrupt his life from day one. Annoyed by the disturbance, he pushes them away until the day he really needs them.

When Daniel gets injured and Macy comes to the rescue, feelings get in the way. Macy agrees to help Daniel until he's recovered but never could have predicted that the arrival of Daniel's ex-fiance would lead to a fake engagement for herself.

Sparks fly when the town gets involved in the fake wedding and Macy and Daniel have to decide what they really want from each other. How far will they take this fake engagement? Can it become real?

ENGAGED TO HER NEIGHBOR
CHAPTER ONE

What is going on? There was a kid in his yard, and a dog too. Daniel headed off his porch to investigate, leaning heavily on his cane. Today was not a good pain day and the last thing he needed to be doing was trekking across the yard in search of answers as to who the wayward dog and child belonged to.

He stopped and rubbed his knee as he made it to the bottom of the steps wincing as the pain shot up his leg before calming back down to its normal dull ache. The worst part was over until it was time to go back inside, stairs made the pain worse, walking more than just around his house was a close second to it.

The dog noticed him before the kid did and stopped chasing the ball and ran straight for Daniel. He braced for impact, but the dog stopped before reaching him and sniffed at him. He took in the yellow, almost white, dog before him. It was gentle, just inquisitive, sniffing him as though sizing him up as well. Daniel stuck his hand out for the dog to sniff and when he felt like he had received approval he patted the dog on the head that was almost reaching his waist and waited for the boy to approach.

~

At least it wasn't raining, that was the only positive part of the day so far. Macy and her brother were supposed to be moving into the new house she had rented them today and everything that could go wrong so far, had. It was more stress than one person should have to deal with.

It all started when she tried to start the rented truck with all their belongings in it, of course the battery was dead. Skipping the costs on roadside assistance had seemed an easy way to save a few bucks, but it just figured she'd need it. Sixty bucks later she had paid someone to come out and jump the battery from the local tow company, and the rest of the day had been much the same. They got a late start, then she had to stop and get food for her and Chris because they had left the peanut butter and jelly sandwiches, that she had packed for them in her car, which of course was at the rental truck place.

The two-hour drive to their new home had been filled with traffic and two complete stops, taking them more than double what it should have. They were so far behind and now she needed to get everything out of the truck so she could return it tomorrow and get her car. She had only taken two days off for this move mentally and needed to get to finding a new job right away, plus she didn't want to pay for an extra day for the rental truck either.

Finally getting to the house which she had rented based off pictures online, she realized there was no way she was going to be able to back the truck down this long, narrow driveway, so now they were adding extra steps to everything. Now Chris had disappeared under the guise of taking Lucy, their lab, for a walk, leaving her to do it all on her own. Chasing him down would waste more time and honestly, he wasn't that much help, one trip to her three, but it was one less thing she had to carry at least.

Sighing, she set down the boxes she had carried in and went in search of Chris and Lucy. Yelling for him, she went through the small one-story house in search of them with no luck. Heading through the back door, she looked out into the yard for them, not seeing them anywhere. She yelled for them and heard Lucy bark, but no one came running. Deciding there was no hope for it, she stepped off the small back porch and went in the direction of the sound.

Looking around, she noticed that the pictures she had seen had done very little justice to the outdoor space here. There was just one neighbor, whose house she could just barely see from hers as it was a good walk away and sat higher than hers on a hill. It was that beautiful green hill that she climbed now. Whoever live here definitely took care of their yard because this was the greenest grass she had ever seen. It took considerable restraint on her part not to take off her shoes and see how it felt under her bare feet.

Smiling and slightly winded, she reached the top of the hill and looked upon a gorgeous two-story house made out of wood. This would be a perfect example of one of those log cabins from the shows on TV where people spend an insane amount of money building a vacation home that they intend to use only a few times a year.

Looking around she spotted Chris and Lucy with a man standing near the woods at the back of their properties. Macy cringed, as she knew how Chris felt about men with the way that their father had treated them. The boy was only eight and should have been running around without a care in the world, instead he was standing there head down, shuffling his feet and listening to the man talk. Lucy noticed her and came running over to greet her and walked with her to Chris.

I hope he hasn't made the new neighbors mad already. I hope that man isn't yelling at him either. Her head swirled with thoughts as she approached them.

The man was dressed in jeans and a solid grey t-shirt and was leaning on a cane with his left hand. He needed a haircut she noticed as she walked closer, it was past the point of touching his ears, but not long enough to be considered long hair. He had a full scruffy beard to match his brown hair that he was reaching up to scratch as she walked up. He looked like an untamed mountain man, one that definitely preferred to be left alone. The look he was giving her now definitely said that he didn't welcome distractions, especially in the form of a rambunctious dog and small boy.

"Hi, I'm Macy, we are moving in next door." She stuck out her hand to greet the man.

"Daniel, and I had guessed as much." He shook her hand. "I hope not to find everyone wandering around in my back yard now that you live here."

"No sir, I will make sure they know where the property line is." She put her hand on Chris's shoulder. "I'm sorry I was unloading the truck and I lost track of them."

The man looked at her. It was more than a look, it was a hard stare, taking her measure and clearly judging her parenting skills, finding them lacking. "See to it that you keep a better eye on them in the future."

With that the man turned and limped away, leaning heavily on his cane. She turned to Chris to fuss at him, but he still had his head down, clearly bothered by running into Daniel on his first day here.

"I'm sorry Macy, I didn't know I wasn't supposed to go this far."

"It's okay bud, you do now. If you had been helping though I would have been able to tell you after we got the truck unloaded."

Chris nodded and then headed down the hill towards their little house. Macy had decided it was in the best interest for both of them to move farther away from their hometown to get away from their father. He was in jail now for hitting a woman while he was driving drunk and injuring her pretty badly. She had lived, but barely. Even though he was locked up and they had nothing to do with it, the stigma of being Joe Manning's kids had followed them around before and had only gotten worse after the accident.

They had been treated as trash their whole lives simply because of parentage and their father hadn't treated them much better. She hadn't called him Dad in so long she had forgotten the last time she had. He wasn't a Dad; Joe was a drunk, and a mean one at that.

Macy's mom had passed away when she was too young to remember her well, then Joe had raised her, if you could call it that. She just remembered being alone all the time, and the endless string of neighbors that used to help watch her until Joe did something to make them stop watching her too. They moved around from trailer park to trailer park, sometimes only staying on someone else's couch because Joe never would hold down a job long.

Then Joe met Candice, or Candy as she was known to everyone else. How they managed to live together for nearly a year was something she never understood. Candy hadn't stuck around long after Chris was born, and then had just disappeared one day. From then on it had been Macy that took care of Chris.

She was only fifteen when he was born, it had made her scared to leave him with Joe while she went to school. Then she had come across an older neighbor that kept Chris for her while she was in school in exchange for Macy cleaning her house and helping her cook meals whenever she could.

It wasn't until she was a few years older and Ms. Mary had passed away that she realized Mary had just been protecting them and teaching Macy all the things that a mom would have taught her. She was their safe harbor in the storm that was their lives and Macy had cried like she had never done before when Ms. Mary had passed away. Joe had refused to take them to the funeral, which had also hurt.

She would have moved out then and tried to make her own way in the world instead of paying bills for Joe, but she couldn't do that to Chris. She had done her absolute best to keep him as sheltered from their father's violent tirades as she could, taking the brunt of his anger, but if she wasn't there anymore, it would all be at Chris.

Shortly after she turned 21, a lawyer contacted her; apparently Mary had a will and had put Macy in it. She had left her a nice sum of money but had decided that she couldn't know of it, or come into it until she was legally old enough to not have to give any to Joe. Ten thousand dollars was a lot of money then and Macy had thought hard about what to do with it.

It had been two years now and she was just reaching out to use it, starting with getting custody of Chris as soon as Joe's trial was over. Then they rented this house, paying for the deposit and a few months rent all at once. It gave her time to get settled into her new job before the big bill of rent was due, which was considerably more than they had been paying at the trailer. They would make it work though; she was sure of it.

They worked until past dark to get the truck unloaded and didn't have time to set anything up. Instead she and Chris curled up on their mattresses on the floor in sleeping bags once everything was in the house. She had found the small cooler with the sandwiches she had made yesterday for today's lunch in the back of the truck, making it so she didn't have to spend more money on food for the night.

She looked over at Chris, curled up with Lucy on his bed, hugging her protectively. She had been the one thing that made Chris feel safe, and she had always done her best to live up to that feeling. Lucy had bitten Joe once on his hand, he had cussed up a storm, but that was the last time he had ever attempted to hit Chris again, for which Macy had been grateful and rewarded Lucy with dinner scraps ever since, she had earned her place in their family.

Macy rolled onto her back and stared up at the ceiling, thinking about this decision. She hoped she could find a job and a sitter within the next two weeks or they were screwed. This plan had been thought out as intensely as she could with the exception of a job, she couldn't make the drive out here for interviews ahead of time, so she prayed that she would find one when Chris started school on Wednesday. With luck it would pay enough for her to only need to work during the day and not require her to get a sitter for after school.

Sleep wouldn't come and after laying there and worrying for too long, she got up and grabbed her cell phone before laying back down. Lucy had lifted her head to watch her but hadn't left Chris's side. Unlocking her phone, she started scrolling through the job postings for Allensville, VA.

MARRIED TO THE PLAYBOY

She wants her happy ending. He wants the girl he can't have. Will fate bring them together?

Kristen likes her life, but she's not in love with it. She knows there's something more out there for her but isn't sure where to look or even if it will make her happy. What she knows for sure is watching her brother marry and begin his happily ever after isn't helping her feel any better about her life.

Mike, a notorious ladies' man, is good at keeping his feelings to himself, but that becomes complicated when he sees his best friend's sister again. Kristen is beautiful, intelligent, and everything he has ever wanted. But when he inadvertently hurts her friend's feelings, Kristen wants nothing to do with him and his playboy ways.

When a fellow teacher backs out of a school fundraising event, Kristen is forced to pull off the biggest event of the year on her own. A friend announces that Mike and Kristen are getting married in front of the town's biggest gossips and another teacher and they must come up with a way out of it, or make a go of things. Mike sees it as an opportunity to make amends and finally win her over, but is the second-grade teacher ready to trust the Army veteran and his past indiscretions?

MARRIED TO THE PLAYBOY
CHAPTER ONE

"You have got to be joking." Kristen only barely stopped herself from stomping her foot.

"It is what it is," Principal Jenkins told her. "The play isn't going to happen unless we get some people in the community to help and a teacher to coordinate it."

"I already do a lot. There are other teachers you could ask to help." She knew she was whining but it seemed every time something needed doing, she was the only one that anyone asked. She also had a hard time saying no and everyone knew it.

"The fifth-grade teachers are busy preparing their graduation, so if we want the annual play to happen, we need someone who knows what needs to be done. You helped Mrs. Kline for two years before she retired, so you know what to do," he explained.

It was true she knew what needed to happen, but that didn't change the fact that she had other things to do already and that she wasn't even the one who volunteered for this in the first place.

"Why can't Beth do it?" Beth, a third-grade teacher, had volunteered to at the beginning of the school year.

Kristen had ended up with the majority of Beth's duties since she started there as a teacher last year. Somehow, she had everyone convinced she was too nice and also too weak to do her own work. Beth hated Kristen though and had ever since they'd met. She had no idea why.

Kristen had asked her once, only for Beth to laugh right in her face, instead of giving her an answer. It was one of very few times that, outside of her brother, Kristen had truly wanted to punch someone, preferably in the face, breaking her perfect little nose.

"Well, she's just really overwhelmed."

Kristen felt her jaw drop. "She quit on it?"

"I didn't say that." He did though, it was written all over his face, if not in his words. "Look, I'm just asking for your help," He took a deep breath and went in for the kill, sealing Kristen's fate, "The kids need your help."

"It's a month away!" She crossed her arms and huffed. "It's not going to be the same as when Mrs. Kline did it; it takes a whole year to plan." A thought crossed her mind, "Beth hasn't done anything, has she?" She pointed her finger at the principal.

"I'm afraid not." Principal Jenkins shook his head. To his credit he did at least look disappointed.

"It'll be different and I don't know what I can pull off."

"I'm just asking that you do your best." He smiled at her before adding, "That's all the kids ask for."

"You've already got me, so you can stop laying it on so thick." Not even trying to stop herself, she rolled her eyes. "She's doing my bus duties for the rest of the year." It was a statement, not a question.

"Now, I don't know if I can have her do it for that—"

Kristen cut him off with a look. "I need time to coordinate all of this." She threw her arms wide.

Nodding, he relented. "Consider it covered."

She put her hand on the doorknob to leave, but had a thought. "This is the only time. I'm going to stop being the teacher here all day every day after this. You better ask the rest of your staff to step up."

She didn't turn around to see his reaction, instead leaving the door open as she walked away. Trying to show power in the conversation that she definitely did not have control over, and also scared that if she turned around he would call her bluff.

It was the end of the school day, so the halls were empty except for a few lingering teachers and staff. Almost always, Kristen was one of the first ones in and definitely one of the last ones out of Springfield Elementary School. Most days she enjoyed the extra things she did, but recently she was growing restless.

It probably had something to do with her brother getting married and having a stepson, with a baby on the way. When she gave herself time to think about it, she realized she was jealous, but she didn't like that, so she didn't give herself much time to think about it.

When she got back to her classroom, she pulled out her phone and called Macy, her sister-in-law.

"Hey girl, I'm not going to make it tonight."

"No, you are not backing out; you need to leave work."

Kristen smiled, thinking of the quiet girl that she'd originally met. Macy had really found herself since getting with Daniel, Kristen's brother. Turned out Macy liked to be in charge and was really good at it.

"I have a new project, doing the entire end-of-year show."

"It can wait until tomorrow. You are coming tonight for dinner."

"Macy, I appreciate it, but I can't."

"Bull. You can and you will; you cancel every time these days."

"Macy—"

"Please, Kristen? We haven't seen you in forever. And I want to talk to you too." She could almost hear Macy's wheels turning, before she continued, "I'll come over and help you with whatever it is tomorrow?"

"I appreciate the offer, but I need to figure out what I am doing first."

"Come on, please?"

"Okay, I will come tonight."

"Yay! You'll feel good to step away from work for a bit."

"I'm not staying long."

"Sure." They both knew she wasn't agreeing to anything though.

Kristen was going to do her best to leave at a decent time to get home and start planning. Sighing as she packed up her work, she knew Macy would convince her to stay, and it wouldn't take much effort even; she needed to work on saying no and holding her ground.

Glancing down at her outfit, she considered going home to change but then dismissed that idea. That would definitely say she planned on being there for a while. Her black pants and paint-stained blouse would have to do.

Despite Beth and all the other stressful things that went along with being a teacher, she loved her kids. It was great seeing the kids grow for the year, and being a second-grade teacher, she got to see the kids grow until the end of fifth grade.

Her class was lively. It annoyed some parents when they found out she didn't have strict desk rules or loads of homework, but that was fine. The kids could sit at a desk, or in a bean bag, or lay on the rug, whatever they needed to do to get the work done. She'd made it through college often laid across her bed, and it had worked well for her.

"Kristen?"

She froze at the voice before turning towards her door. Beth was standing there looking as freshly put together as she had at the beginning of the day. Clearly not a stressful Friday for her. Not a platinum-blonde hair out of place, high heels clicking across the hard floor as she walked in, her black pencil skirt and nearly see-through blouse were just this side of respectable.

"Can I help you?" Kristen asked and then mentally kicked herself. She didn't want to help Beth with anything, definitely the wrong question to ask.

"I'm glad you asked." The smile was sweet but Beth's blue eyes held contempt. "I heard you wanted me to take your bus duties, and I just can't."

"Excuse me?" That was it? Just can't? *We aren't even going to make up an excuse anymore?*

"Yeah, you'll need to keep doing them." She started walking away.

"Why not?" Kristen asked.

"I have personal reasons." Beth gave a little smile, but it wasn't friendly.

"You expect me to do all of your work?"

Beth laughed her sweet, fake, feminine laugh and didn't answer as she walked away. Kristen wanted to yell out in frustration but didn't. She opened her top desk drawer and pulled out a self-help book about learning to say no and added it to her bag.

"This weekend I will read you," she thought out loud as she picked her bag up and left the school.

She was all the way to her car before she wondered why dinner was so important tonight. The car was in gear and she was on her way there before she allowed herself to admit there was only one reason why Macy would push so hard.

"Mike," she said before groaning. Not one to curse normally, there was only one word to sum up the situation: "Shit."

It was definitely going to be a long night and Macy better have thought to grab some wine, because that was the only way Kristen was going to get through it.

READ MORE

Checkout the start to the Westbeach Series by turning the page!

OLD FRIENDS PREVIEW

Chapter 1

Taking in the scenery, Kelly wondered why she never came back to visit. Going home was hard, but it was only about a four-hour drive. She really should have come home before now. Taking the long road around the outside of town, the scenery alternated between trees so dense the automatic headlights came on in her car and open pastures with cows or horses in them. This time of year, everything was still bright green. It looked pretty, but she knew better; being late August, it was hot out there. Soon the brilliant green would give way to a wonder of colors as fall slowly crept in.

Turning the music down, she focused on the GPS and the last few miles of her trip. Traffic had started to pick up in the previous hour of her journey until she left the interstate. She was glad she had left earlier in the day; it was only about 4:00 p.m. now. A quick check of the back seat showed Hunter was waking up. For a seven-year-old, he wasn't a bad road-trip partner, but he had slept all but the first hour, when he ate most of the snacks. "Hey, Hunt, we're almost there. Are you excited?"

"Are we in a zoo?" Hunter sleepily asked.

Kelly took another look around, wondering why this was even a question. Cows. There were cows on both sides of the road. "No, baby, there are ranches around here that raise cows."

"So, I'll see the zoo every day?"

"Yes." Simpler to agree than to explain more as he wasn't awake yet. Besides, in all his seven years, he'd never seen the countryside, and Westbeach was about as opposite of DC as you could get.

As they made the last turn, the woods on either side were a welcome presence, adding shade to the last bit of the trip, which had been mostly on the sunny highway. She was going to have a sunglasses tan for sure. Finally pulling in to the driveway, Kelly breathed a sigh of relief to see her aunt and uncle already there and waiting for them.

The light blue house was one level and had a small new porch on the front. The wood was still white looking, so she could tell it hadn't been there long. The front yard was freshly cut, and there were trees on both sides of the property and behind it. A privacy fence, which also looked new, wrapped around the backyard. No neighbors could be seen unless you were in the road. *Wonder if I'll be able to sleep without the noise of the city?*

Aunt Mary was the first to come off the porch as Kelly parked the car. Mary, in her signature flower dress and floppy hat over her white hair, had always been able to style anything except herself. Her dresses were like something older ladies probably wore in the fifties. Gardening, cooking, shopping—same dresses; some things never changed. Bob, on the other hand, was a jeans and T-shirt man. Kelly could never remember Uncle Bob having hair—on his head or face. Much like Mary though, his style was the same no matter what he was doing. The only thing these two changed was the colors each day.

When Kelly stepped out of her car, Aunt Mary immediately wrapped her in a welcoming hug. "How are you doin', dear? How was the trip?"

"Let her get out of the car, Mary." Uncle Bob always sounded a tad sour but was a sweetheart underneath.

"I am, I am." Aunt Mary backed up and opened the back door for

Hunter to climb out of the car. "Hunter! You've gotten so big!" Hunter grinned and stood tall at her praise. Mary ruffled his hair and proceeded to go to the trunk with Uncle Bob to get their bags. "Is this all you brought, honey?"

"For now. The rest is packed, and Dylan is supposed to send it this week, but we'll see if he remembers to let the movers in or not."

"Okay, let us know if you forgot anything." Aunt Mary smiled sadly at Kelly.

"You know I will." She plastered on a big smile to reassure everyone that she really was okay. Taking Hunter's hand, she turned and walked into the house.

When she walked in, the first thing she noticed was that the house was fully furnished; some things even looked new. A gray sofa in the living room faced a flat-screen TV with a small coffee table. Passing through the living room to the kitchen, she noticed there was a cherry-colored table for four with a bouquet of fresh flowers waiting for them. *Definitely Aunt Mary's idea.* And the smell—some version of every spice, but in a good way—was just like Bob and Mary's house. It was a welcoming scent, the smell of home.

Kelly walked down the hall of the modest one-story house, pulling her suitcase behind her. Three rooms, two bathrooms—per Mary's directions, hers was the last on the left. The room had a large queen-sized bed in the center with a gorgeous purple quilt and matching pillows on it. A dresser sat against the long wall with a mirror attached.

Checking all the doors, she discovered the closet was behind the open bedroom door, and against the wall was a master bath. A purple shower curtain hung already with silver bath mats. Aunt Mary really should have been an interior designer, and her remembering Kelly's favorite color just made it that much better.

Kelly had never been able to have everything decorated in her favorite color before, but now she could do her thing. Putting her bag down she took a deep breath; divorce wasn't going to be too bad if this was how it started. Coming back home wasn't all that bad, even if it did make her feel a little like a failure for her marriage not working.

There was no love lost in her marriage anyway. Dylan didn't even fight for custody of Hunter. He just let them go and agreed to everything—not that she had asked for much, just child support and custody. Dylan didn't even want weekends with Hunter. Kelly sighed as she looked in the mirror and pulled her hair into a ponytail before heading back out to the other three noisily chatting about cows in the dining room.

"Hunter tells me he's excited to see the zoo every day," Uncle Bob informed her with a laugh as he pulled Kelly up for a quick hug. Although pushing seventy, Bob was still a tall man. He was the exact opposite of Mary, who was shorter than Kelly by five inches, standing at five feet tall. The family had always joked that it was her hat that gave her an inch or two and that she genuinely was less than five feet. Mary had always laughed along as well, shushing everyone, but never argued it.

"Something tells me he'll eventually tire of it," Kelly said with a small laugh of her own.

"I stocked some essentials in the cabinets and fridge; wasn't sure what all you would need. We can go to dinner later, or you can come over and I'll cook." Aunt Mary always made sure everyone had eaten. If you weren't hungry, she was going to have you doing something until you were. "We are waiting on the handyman though. The disposal isn't working right now."

"No problem, and we can eat whatever is easiest for you tonight. Thank you guys again." Bending down, she hugged Aunt Mary again and gave her a kiss on the cheek. "I don't know what I would do without you guys here."

"Family helps family, dear." And that was all Aunt Mary was going to say about it. No thanks needed ever.

"I love you." Before either of them did more than tear up, Kelly changed the subject. "The handyman? Is that who redid the front porch? It looks nice."

"Yes, yes. Bob thought he was going to do it. Took the boards off and then decided it was too much for one old man, like I said." She cut a look at Bob, who decided not to say anything and continued to talk to Hunter. "Thankfully," Mary continued, "the handyman was able to get out here and get it done before you got here."

"Really?" Hunter shouted and jumped up from the table to run out the back door.

"I told him there was a swing set out there." Bob smiled and moved to follow Hunter out the door.

"He will never come inside again." Kelly laughed and moved to the window to see Hunter happily swinging while Uncle Bob looked on.

"Go unpack, and I'll wait right here for the doorbell," Mary said while shooing Kelly from the window. "He'll be fine."

"I know. I'll be in his room for now if you need me."

Wandering down the hall, Kelly opened the door across from her room and was pleased to find an office. Mary really had thought of everything. A small desk sat facing the window with a fancy-looking high-backed office chair, and she could see the entire backyard from there. A tall lamp in the corner would keep her from having to turn on the overhead light to see, and a ceiling fan was a nice addition. The room was painted a darker shade of blue, but it didn't seem to make the room feel smaller.

There was plenty of room left in there for her treadmill since there was no gym here that she knew of, and going for a run would be difficult with Hunter still home for the summer. Mary always knew what worked and what didn't without even trying. Kelly would be glad to get back to work in two weeks in her new office. Thankfully, her legal transcription was work from home, and they had been generous with her time off under the circumstances. She would have a pile of work when she got back to it though. It was going to be rough going back to work after all this time off. Thinking about her emails that she hadn't checked all day, she walked out of the room and closed the door.

Moving on, Kelly checked the room next to hers and saw a twin bed, some toys already set out for Hunter, and a large baseball poster on the wall across from her. Smiling, she walked over and touched it, amazed by the little things Bob and Mary had thought of to help

Hunter adjust. She'd also bet money that there was no swing set here before Kelly decided to move in. Kelly heaved Hunter's suitcase on the bed and started to unpack and put away the clothes.

"I didn't pack hangers." Kelly let out a deep sigh. "If this is the worst part, I'm good, right?" Musing to herself, she walked down the hall to see if Mary wanted to go to the store. "Mary, are you interested in running to the—" Seeing a man in the kitchen, Kelly stopped midsentence.

"Kelly, this is Mason, the handyman. Mason, do you remember Kelly?"

"How could I forget?" Drying his hands off, he looked up, and Kelly stared into eyes she hadn't seen in twelve years. Mason Cole.

"Wow! How are you? It's been forever." Not sure what to do with herself, she leaned awkwardly against the wall, taking in this man who had been a teenager when she saw him last. Instead, here was this man with his dark brown hair and muscles she could see through his blue shirt. And those blue eyes... a woman could get lost in those eyes. He hadn't changed much other than getting older, like her she supposed. He was still as handsome as ever.

"How's the set working out?" Mason interrupted Kelly's assessment of him. Oh, that smile, crooked with one dimple on the right cheek. That smile could make women fall all over themselves to get a glimpse of it. Nope, that hadn't changed one bit.

"Hunter is already out there." Mary saved her from having to form an answer. Nothing could have prepared Kelly for seeing this man in her kitchen.

Swallowing down old feelings and trying to move forward, Kelly shifted to look out the window on the back door to see Hunter still outside playing. Taking it in for the first time, she noticed the back deck was only slightly above ground level, just one step up. *I need to get a table and chairs for out here, so I can work and watch Hunter play.* The yard was a fair size, plenty of room for Hunter to run around, and the start of the tree line had been fenced into the yard, giving him a shaded place to play. The swing set was a good size as well, containing two swings, a slide, and monkey bars on one end. Uncle

Bob strolled from the deck to the yard, watching Hunter wear himself out. *At least he'll sleep tonight, even after that long nap in the car.*

"What did you need, dear?" Aunt Mary asked.

"Oh, I didn't pack hangers and was wondering where the closest store was?" She focused on Mary, anything to not stare at this too-hot-to-be-here man in the kitchen.

"That would still be Gersham's down on Main Street. I have to head there to order the part for your disposal if you'd like a ride?" Of course, it was Mason who answered. And a ride, really? Lord knew she wanted to go for a ride. Wait, where had that thought come from? How unlike her; must be the nerves.

"I don't want to impose. I can head down there later."

"No imposing at all. Grab your bag and hop in the truck." Interesting how the words he chose said he made the decision, but the tone made it clear it was still her call.

Grabbing her bag, she let Hunter know she would be right back. For all he cared though, he was still enthralled with the swings and slide out back. After hugging Aunt Mary, she walked out to the dark blue Dodge Ram sitting in her driveway. Mason was standing by the truck and opened the door for her. He waited until she had settled before closing it. *What am I supposed to say now? What do I do?* Placing her bag in her lap, she sat still as he climbed in and backed out the driveway. Not much was said on the way to the store.

Staring out the passenger window, she watched the scenery. Everything seemed the same, and yet it all seemed so different at the same time. When they got to the store, they went their separate ways after Mason pointed her in the right direction. She grabbed several packs of hangers and headed toward the checkout. Mason was already standing there putting in an order for whatever part it was he needed.

As she approached, a shiver ran down her spine. Kelly felt like someone was watching her. Looking around, she didn't see anyone else in the store besides Mason and the clerk. Still, she picked up her pace, unable to shake the creepy feeling. She set the hangers on the counter, continuing to look around while waiting for them to finish.

You're losing it. No one is in here, just the empty store getting you creeped out.

Needing a distraction, she watched the interaction going on at the register. The woman was practically hanging on Mason's every word like she was super interested in garbage disposals. Kelly rolled her eyes. When she looked up again, Mason winked at her. She had been caught. Completely distracted from the creepy feeling, she now had a new one—full-on embarrassment.

Part ordered and hangers paid for, they walked back to the truck again. Mason took the awkward bags of hangers and opened her door for her. While Kelly buckled in, he put the bags in the back seat, then shut her door and got in.

"Didn't like her much, did you?"

Kelly felt the heat creep up her face. He wasn't going to ignore her eye roll. "It wasn't that. More of a disbelief type of thing." *There, that makes me sound less rude for not liking someone I don't even know and positively not jealous.*

"Nope, it's been a while, but you still can't hide anything. It's all over your face," he teased.

Kelly put her hand to her heart and leaned toward Mason, doing an exaggerated impersonation of the busty clerk. "Oh, please tell me more about garbage disposals." She batted her lashes. "I just don't know what I would do without you having come in today, Mason." Kelly laughed and sat back right in the seat.

"Pretty good impression actually. Now you know why I didn't want to go to the store alone." Mason cut her a sly look but laughed as well. After a moment, they both fell into a companionable silence for the rest of the trip. Pulling up, Mason stopped her from opening the door with a hand on her shoulder. "It's good to see you and have you home again, even if it's not under the best of circumstances."

"Thank you. I'm glad to be home. No love lost in the reason for my coming home, so no worries. I'm glad I got to see you."

"If you need anything while you're here, let me give you my number. Your aunt and uncle call when something needs to be done in one of their rentals. Most of your new home has been newly renovated though; they really went all out to make it right for you. Oh, and I'll let Bob know when the part comes in. She said Tuesday, but when I pick it up will depend on when I can get someone to go to the store with me." Mason laughed again.

"I noticed. The porch looks great, and the swing set too. If you let me know when the part is ready, I can run in and pick it up, and then you can avoid the store altogether." Kelly winked at him. "You can just let me know. Let me find a paper, and I'll give you my number." She dug through her bag and came up with a crayon and a receipt. Blushing again at how much of a mess she must seem, she wrote her number down and handed it to him. Saying their goodbyes, she hopped out of the truck and went inside with a smile on her face.

\#

Kelly Marie Holstead, he didn't know she would be there today. He could have sworn it was tomorrow that Mary said she would get here. Pulling into his own driveway, he smiled as he remembered Kelly's reaction to Darlene, the clerk at Gersham's. Just like the old Kelly would have done, she let loose with that cute little eye roll. Heading inside, he greeted Shep, his aging yellow lab, with a pat on the head. Shep followed him through the house, waiting to be let outside. Grabbing a beer from the fridge, Mason opened the back door and went out to the deck, Shep in tow.

Checking his phone, he texted Nate, his brother and business partner, about the disposal and the part needed. He pulled Kelly's crayon-written number out of his pocket and plugged it into his phone. *Should I text her now, so she has my number? Is it too soon?* After deciding to just program the number in and debate it later, his thoughts wandered to the day he had. After a rough morning with two young guys late to work, again, he was frustrated and cranky when he remembered he was supposed to check on Kelly's disposal today. When he pulled up, he was in no mood for small talk with Mary but had resigned himself to it. Then he noticed another car in the driveway.

Kelly apparently hadn't been expecting him. He wasn't entirely expecting her either. He hadn't seen her in almost twelve years, since they were seventeen and about to graduate high school. That summer was some of the best memories he had though. Kelly was his best friend, but when they went to college in different states, they had slowly lost touch. It was one of his biggest regrets. He and Kelly had shared everything—sometimes too much, but he could always tell her anything, and she, him. He knew Kelly had gotten married right after she graduated college, and that was about it.

She still looked as good as ever, a more mature woman and no longer the body of a teenager, but time had been kind to her. Her blonde hair had been pulled back, but it was more than shoulder length and had some highlights. Her body though, she looked like she took care of herself; he could see her defined leg muscles under her shorts. Her curves were more significant than he remembered. She wore no makeup, probably not something she usually did, but no reason to get dolled up for a road trip to move. He liked the no makeup look though, no pretending, nothing to hide.

Just then his phone went off, pulling him out of his thoughts as they headed in the wrong direction. Texting Nate back, he got up, adjusted his pants, and Shep followed him in the door. Nate was going to give him a hard time about seeing Kelly, and about venturing into Gersham's when he knew Darlene would be working. He wasn't kidding; he had taken Kelly as a bit of a buffer. Darlene always shamelessly threw herself at him, but she'd limit it to flirting if there was someone else in the store. The woman never took the hint that he wasn't interested, even though he had tried to let her down gently many times before. Now he just avoided the place when he knew she was working.

Time to make dinner. Pulling out the chicken, he got started on cooking. *Wonder if she still cooks as well as she used to?* What the hell was he doing, thinking about her so much? It had only been a few minutes, and nothing had even happened to make him feel so much about her. She hadn't thrown herself at him like most women, so what was it?

Finishing up dinner, he carried it to the living room. Watching TV would distract his wayward thoughts.

\#

He waited in his car with the lights off until Mason had finally left Kelly's house. He had watched her from the back of the store as she searched hangers. He couldn't believe she had been home just a few hours and was already back with Mason. How had that happened? Had to be her meddling aunt. He had been watching the house for the past week waiting for her arrival and would meet her again soon. She was supposed to come back after she finished school, and like a fool, he had expected her to, but no, she went and got married and hadn't come back at all.

He had followed her online for a long time and had made sure she found out about her husband's cheating. Chuckling to himself, he remembered how easy that had been. He had just pretended to be the secretary's doctor and called their house phone looking for the father of the baby. Of course, Kelly had answered. Then he "accidentally" spilled the news of the baby to her. He had gotten her home now. She hadn't been happy in her marriage anyway, so he didn't feel bad. This time, she would be his, and neither Mason nor anything else was going to stand in his way. He carefully put away his phone, excited to have new photos of her on it, and headed home.

ABOUT THE AUTHOR

Toni Denise lives in southeastern Virginia with her husband, four kids, and three dogs. She loves to read as much as she loves to write. She has three degrees including an MBA is project management and works full time in human resources. Don't worry, she knows none of that goes together.

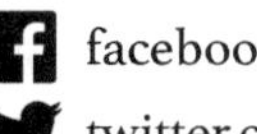 facebook.com/ToniDeniseAuthor
 twitter.com/tonidenisebooks
instagram.com/toni_denise_author